ON THE RUN 1

CHASING
THE
FALCONERS

GORDON KORMAN

SCHOLASTIC

First published in the UK in 2007 by Scholastic Children's Books
An imprint of Scholastic Ltd
Euston House, 24 Eversholt Street, London, NW1 1DB, UK
Registered office: Westfield Road, Southam, Warwickshire, CV47 0RA
SCHOLASTIC and associated logos are trademarks and or registered trademarks
of Scholastic Inc.

First published in the US in 2005 by Scholastic, Inc.,
Text copyright © Gordon Korman, 2005
The right of Gordon Korman to be identified as the author of this work
has been asserted by him.
Cover illustration by David Wyatt, 2007

10 digit ISBN 0 439 94386 8
13 digit ISBN 978 0439 94386 4

A CIP catalogue record for this book is available from the British Library.

Printed by Bookmarque Ltd, Croydon, Surrey
Papers used by Scholastic Children's Books are made from wood grown in
sustainable forests.

1 3 5 7 9 10 8 6 4 2

www.scholastic.co.uk/zone

In memory of the irreplaceable
Paula Danziger

It wasn't a prison.

Not technically, anyway.

No bars, cells, electrified fencing, guard towers, or razor wire.

People who drove by probably never noticed the logo of the Department of Juvenile Corrections on the mailbox that stood at the end of the long lane leading to County Road 413. To them, this sprawling property was just another farm – one of thousands of dusty puzzle pieces that covered this part of Nebraska.

Farm. Aiden Falconer winced. He hated that word. Sunnydale Farm, they called it – a name so deliberately cheerful it turned his stomach.

His eyes took in the empty, far-flung acreage. This broad, flat land wasn't meant for crops. It was a barrier. Anybody trying to escape would have to cross that pool-table-flat boundary in full view of the supervisors, for too many miles and too many minutes. It was as effective as a moat full of alligators.

Welcome to Alcatraz Junior.

True, there were a few farmy things. A modest cornfield and a few acres of soybeans. Busy work for the "residents".

Inmates, Aiden thought bitterly.

Life at Sunnydale Farm was based on one simple principle: that the residents could not be allowed so much as a second of free time. For these juvenile offenders, time meant trouble.

So there was school. Seven hours, broken only by a twenty-minute Gulp 'n' Gag lunch. The rest of each day, from five a.m. wake-up until lights-out at nine, the eighteen boys and twelve girls worked the "farm" – tilling, planting, fertilizing, pruning and picking. They tended the chickens and fought with the geese.

And they milked the cows.

Aiden hated milking duty almost as much as he hated Sunnydale itself, and his reason for being there. OK, animals weren't clean freaks, but that barn stank to high heaven and was hot as a sauna. To enter it was to stop breathing until the chore was done and you could stagger out, blue in the face and gasping for air.

Milking was an art that he seemed incapable of mastering. Some of the residents could plunk themselves down on the stool, reach under the cow, and you'd hear *squirt, squirt, squirt*. Aiden would plaster his face against the flank of the beast, his hands working like pistons. The *squirt, squirt, squirt* never came.

The frustration was maddening. He was a Falconer, from a family known for its brains. His parents were both PhDs. Respected scientists.

Or at least they used to be. . .

No. Don't go there.

The cow was losing patience with Aiden's incompetence. It happened just the way it always did. First the twitching. In a few seconds, it would turn its massive head and moo at him. Next, the shuffling and stamping. And then the kick. He would go one way, the stool would go the other, and the pail would be upended, spilling into the straw of the stall the few drops he had managed to squeeze out.

His escape came a split second before the cow went into total revolt. Aiden jumped up and fled the barn, feeling sick and breathless, his tan jumpsuit drenched with sweat.

"What a wuss." Miguel Reyes walked towards the

henhouse, carrying a sack of chicken feed. "Nobody's scared of cows. Dumbest animals on the planet – next to *you*."

As he passed by, he made sure to whack Aiden on the side of the head with the heavy bag.

"Ow!"

"Are you OK?" Meg Falconer peered anxiously around the corner of the barn.

Aiden could never quite get used to the sight of his eleven-year-old sister in this terrible place. At fifteen, he was as old as most of the juvenile offenders banished to this prison camp. But Meg was just a kid, ripped out of sixth grade.

"Beat it!" he hissed at her. Boys and girls were supposed to stay separated except during classes and Gulp 'n' Gag.

Meg had never been big on following rules. She usually got by on a sweet smile and wide-eyed innocence – all fake.

"Are you going to let him get away with that?" she demanded.

Aiden stared at her. "This isn't some self-esteem game about standing up to bullies. That guy was in Juvie before this. For *manslaughter*!"

"But where does it stop?" she demanded. "Mom and Dad – framed! The two of us, stuck away in the back of beyond! We don't even know who we *are* any more."

"If I pick a fight with Miguel," Aiden warned, "I'll know *exactly* who I am. I'll be the dead guy in the morgue!"

"Hey!" came an angry shout.

The supervisor who stormed over was named Ray. The residents called him Rage because he was always in one. In Aiden's opinion, that nickname could have gone to any of the other jailers at Sunnydale. There was a kind of permanent anger in the people who worked there — probably from dealing with delinquents like Miguel day in and day out. The "supes" got sassed so often that they lived in a constant state of being bent out of shape.

Ray was scowling as usual. "Well, what do you know — Eagleson and Eagleson. A regular family reunion."

Eagleson — that was their identity at Sunnydale. Falcon, eagle — like this was some kind of April Fools' prank. The court had ordered the change. After the media circus of their parents' trial, *Falconer* might as well have been *Dracula* as a last name. The judge said he didn't want the children suffering for their parents' crimes.

If this isn't suffering, then what is? Aiden wondered

5

angrily. *We're banished to this Old-McDonald-Had-a-Jail, mingling with dangerous offenders. While Mom and Dad rot in prison for something they didn't even do —*

He took a breath. The Falconer kids were at Sunnydale because none of their relatives would take them in. Who could blame the distant cousins for wanting to shield their own families from the scandal? A day didn't go by without Mom and Dad decried as traitors in every newspaper in the country.

Aiden and Meg had committed no crime. They were here because there was no other place for them.

"Sorry, Ray. It won't happen again—"

His sister cut him off. "That's funny, Ray. You're quick enough to catch us talking. But someone using a sack of feed as a deadly weapon – you missed that, didn't you?"

The supervisor's scowl deepened. "You little snot, how'd you like to lose your telephone privileges for a month?"

That shut Meg up. Those weekly phone calls were the only contact the Falconer kids had with their parents in prison in Florida.

All the contact we'll ever have...

Luckily, Meg had the brains not to fight with a

supe. She retreated to her work in the soybean fields, and Aiden steeled himself for round two with the cows.

But later, as he was returning his tray after Gulp 'n' Gag, Meg stepped out in front of him, her eyes like lasers. She grabbed both his wrists with such intensity that it took all his strength to keep the dishes and cutlery from sliding to the floor.

"We have to get out of here," she murmured urgently.

"Get a grip," he whispered back. "There's no way out of this place."

"We *have* to!" she insisted. "We're Mom and Dad's only chance."

For a second, he thought he might start losing it right there in the mess. Wouldn't *that* show Miguel and the others how tough he was. "The appeal—"

She shook her head fervently. "The government will never let them go. The case is closed. We're the only ones who can prove our parents are innocent, and you know it!"

Classic Meg. She didn't live in the real world. Escape was impossible. But even if they could get away, then what? How would two kids come up with evidence that would clear the Falconers after so many top lawyers had failed?

And then there was the question he dreaded most of all. The unthinkable thought, the one he dared not ever speak aloud, even to his own sister.

What if he and Meg set out to exonerate their parents, only to discover that they had been guilty all along?

"Dude, your house is on TV!"

With those six words in the school hall, the nightmare had begun.

A group of students had gathered around the wall-mounted screen in the media centre. The sound was muted, but Aiden could see it — his own front door.

His first thought was idiotic: *New paint job still looking good. . .*

Not *What's going on?* or *Why is my house on CNN?* The paint job.

The camera pulled back, and he saw the police. More like an *army*. Scores of commandos in body armour surrounded the Falconer home, shields deployed, weapons pointed. A roadblock cut off their quiet street. Choppers circled overhead.

What the—?

The rest was a blur. Exploding tear gas canisters. The battering ram reducing the door to toothpicks.

His parents hustled out in handcuffs by an FBI agent the size of Shaquille O'Neal.

And then the call over the PA: "Would Aiden Falconer please come to the main office? Aiden Falconer. . ."

Like things were totally normal. Like they were going to tell him that Mom had forgotten to sign his field-trip form.

That was March 7. The day the world ended. The day life changed for ever for Aiden and Meg.

The details came twenty-one hours later. At long last, they were allowed to see their parents in a windowless maximum-security cell guarded by two soldiers armed with automatic rifles.

The charge: passing classified information to enemies of the state.

"Classified information?" Aiden stared at his father. "What would you be doing with classified information? You're a teacher at a college nobody's ever heard of! And you write detective novels!"

"*Bad* detective novels," Meg added breathlessly.

The Falconers told their story. Husband and wife professors – both respected criminologists. Three years before, they had been approached by an old family friend who turned out to be an undercover CIA recruiter. Their country needed their expertise,

Agent Frank Lindenauer told them, in the global war on terror.

For the next eighteen months, the two professors worked for the government. They developed profiles for United States operatives to identify terrorist sleeper cells throughout the world. It was going beautifully, Lindenauer assured them. Thanks to the Falconers' work, the CIA had the foreign extremists on the run.

And then everything fell apart.

Somehow, the Falconer profiles had fallen into the hands of the terrorists themselves. Knowing what the Americans were looking for had surely helped them avoid capture.

Now the Department of Homeland Security accused the two criminologists of aiding the enemies of their country. The crime was treason.

"So?" wailed Meg. "Just get Frank Whatsisface to explain that you're the good guys!"

That was the problem: Agent Frank Lindenauer had disappeared off the face of the earth.

For months, the Falconers and their lawyers tried to reach him, with no success. Worse, the CIA claimed it employed no such operative. He was the professors' only contact — the one person who could back up their story.

During the trial, witness after witness detailed how the Falconers' work had become a training manual for sleeper agents. Captured extremists testified that the profiles were widely used in the terrorist world.

Without their CIA handler, the Falconers had no way to defend themselves. It was over before it started. But the sentence was beyond their wildest nightmares:

"You are remanded to the custody of the Department of Corrections for a term of not less than the length of your natural lives."

The gavel came down like a pistol shot. It was a moment that happened on television a dozen times a day. But TV never showed the real story – the shattered lives, the ruined families.

What happens to a son and daughter when two loving parents are suddenly shut away for good?

At least the juvenile authorities got one thing right: they kept Aiden and Meg together. Mom and Dad weren't so lucky.

The foster homes were a disaster – accusations and fighting on the inside and encampments of reporters on the lawn. Falconer wasn't a name any more; it was a glowing neon sign. After a few false starts, the judge decided that the only option was to get these kids out of the spotlight. They had to disappear, taking their notorious pedigree with them.

That's Sunnydale, Aiden thought bitterly. *The place you go when you want to be nowhere.*

Gang members, purse snatchers and car thieves made great camouflage.

The TV was barely watchable, with faded colour and a jumping picture. Yet to the boys of Sunnydale, it was Disney World – their only entertainment besides bragging, threatening and fighting. The two fuzzy channels were their sole connection to the world that lay beyond the endless fields.

Nowhere was the pecking order more obvious than around the TV. At six foot four, Latrell Chambers was able to claim for himself the only halfway comfortable chair. It didn't hurt his reputation as a tough guy that he used to belong to an infamous Seattle gang. Miguel was right up there, too, on a lumpy couch with a great viewing angle. Gary Donovan – armed robbery – had a beanbag chair that he defended with both fists. And so on down to Aiden, pretty close to rock bottom – obstructed view of a picture that was pretty obstructed to begin with. Only Seth Lowinger, computer hacker, had less status. He didn't watch TV at all.

Aiden wondered what the atmosphere was like in the girls' lounge. Was his eleven-year-old sister subjected to this kind of ugliness and intimidation? With Mom and Dad out of the game, Aiden had to stand up for Meg. But how could he do that when he could barely stand up for himself?

A half-eaten pear came sailing through the air and knocked the old-fashioned rabbit-ear antenna off the top of the set. Instantly, the picture dissolved into snow, and a howl went up from the spectators.

Gary Donovan smacked Miguel on the back of the head. "What's the matter with you, Reyes? It took us weeks to get that stupid thing exactly right!"

Miguel tossed his wadded-up napkin at the blank screen. "For what, yo? To watch reruns of *Touched by an Angel*? When I get out of here, I'm going to kick back with my brother in New Jersey. He's got, like, seven hundred channels, plasma screen, satellite dish, the works! That's for me."

"Dream on," sneered Latrell. "They're never going to let you out of here – not till you turn twenty-one, anyway."

Aiden waited for the explosion and fist fight, but Miguel just laughed.

"This cage can't hold me," he boasted. "I'm just chilling, that's all."

There was a lot of hooting and jeering, and Miguel was pelted with apple cores and candy wrappers.

Aiden spoke up. "You know a way out?"

Miguel snorted in his face. "Look at the big escape artist! You don't have the guts to milk a cow, Eagledink. You'd wet your pants before you hit the cornfield."

"Shut up, Reyes," snorted Gary. "There's no way out, and you know it. Not unless you can walk thirty miles in a Juvie jumpsuit without being seen."

"That's why you guys are a bunch of felons," said Miguel. "No creativity. Look around you. You see a cage. I see wood, and hay, and papers. One match, and this whole dump *burns*."

Gary opened his eyes wide. "You want to *torch* the place? And escape while the supes are manning the bucket brigade?"

Latrell gave an uninterested yawn. "You're talking nonsense, man. You've got a rap sheet like the *En-cyclopaedia Britannica*. Slap an arson on there, and they'll put you in the adult system no matter how old you are."

Miguel shrugged. "Gotta catch me first." He waved at Aiden. "Hey, Eagledink, go fix the antenna. And get it right this time."

15

Aiden did as he was told, but he never took his eyes off Miguel. "You're kidding about that, right? The fire? That can't work, can it?"

Miguel chuckled his contempt. "What are you in for, Eagle? Spitting on the sidewalk? Jaywalking? I know everybody's sheet in this place except you and your little sis. What did you do – whack your parents or something?"

Suddenly, there was nothing more important to Aiden than taking the antenna and ramming it down Miguel's throat. He was on the boy like a flying squirrel, almost screaming with rage.

What happened next was shocking and lightning fast. Miguel shrugged him off as easily as he might have flicked away a crumb. The punches were airborne like missiles, compact, bony fists slamming into Aiden's cheek and chin.

Aiden tasted blood and prepared himself to shed more. *I don't belong with these criminals,* he thought with amazing detachment. *How can I ever hope to defend myself against them?*

Latrell grabbed Miguel by the back of his collar and hauled him off Aiden. "Cut it out, fool! You want the supes on our necks?"

Gary hauled Aiden to his feet, but his real concern

16

was for the antenna, which was bent like a pretzel. "Aw, man, you broke it!"

Somehow, the TV picture was now clearer than it had ever been. That, Aiden assumed, was the only reason why he was allowed to go on living.

The incident did nothing to improve relations with Miguel. "You'd better watch your back, Eagledink," he promised grimly. "When you least expect it, this is the face that's going to be coming up behind you."

If there was a force that could overpower Aiden's anger and resentment at the fate that had overtaken his family, it was sheer boredom. The routine at Sunnydale was so repetitive, so dull, that days slipped into weeks, and weeks slipped into months without anybody noticing how much of life was being wasted.

It had been over four months since the Falconers' arrival at the farm. The corn was getting higher and the days were getting shorter. Other than that, there was very little indication that time was passing at all.

Even the changes didn't seem like changes in the great numbness that was Sunnydale. Gary completed his term and was released. The very next day, his replacement showed up. Eugene from Boston, aggravated assault. He looked and acted exactly like Gary and even inherited Gary's spot in the pecking order and seat at the TV.

Last Wednesday, Aiden and Meg had spoken to

their father in prison in Florida. Dr Falconer had tried to sound upbeat. "Hang in there, kids. You won't be in that place for ever."

Meg had cried, and Aiden had come pretty close himself. The awful flip side of that statement was obvious: Dad would be in *his* jail for ever, and Mom in hers. Life meant life.

Every night at Sunnydale, two residents were selected to see to the animals' food and water supplies overnight and into the morning. Turndown service, the supervisors called it.

Aiden found no humour in their gag. The duty was creepy in the extreme. There was no electricity in any of the outbuildings, so the barn and coops were pitch-black.

Aiden entered the gloom of the henhouse, holding up the kerosene lantern, leading the way for Seth Lowinger, his partner tonight. The hens stirred as the intruders passed from roost to roost, filling water cups and feed trays.

Seth, whose crime was creating a high-tech computer virus that had shut down every ATM in eleven states, couldn't figure out how to open a sack of chicken feed.

"You just tear it, Seth," Aiden told him. "Where the stitching is."

"I don't see any stitching," Seth complained. "What – over here? It won't tear."

Aiden bit back a sarcastic remark. He would not become like Miguel and the others and make fun of someone who was even lower on the totem pole than he was.

He set the lantern down on the floor and ripped open the heavy paper. As he handed the feed back to Seth, the bottom of the bag knocked over the kerosene lamp. The little glass door fell open, and the flame licked out to the straw-strewn floor.

Aiden quickly dropped to his knees to beat out the small fire. All at once, Miguel's words echoed in his ears: *One match and this whole dump burns. . .*

Suddenly, he was frozen, staring transfixed at the fingers of flame rising from the parched-dry hay.

"Hey!" cried Seth. "*Hey!*"

It jolted Aiden out of his reverie. But by the time he moved to put out the fire, there was no stopping it. Miguel had been right. The farm was a tinderbox.

Aiden pounded at the flames with the feed bag, but the blaze was spreading faster than he could stamp it out, accelerated by the spilled kerosene.

A tinderbox . . . a tinderbox. . .

There was nothing in here that would contain a

fire. In a matter of seconds, half the floor was burning.

Seth was in a full-blown panic. "It's going up the walls!"

The sensation that overtook Aiden was like waking from semi-consciousness into terrifying reality. This was nothing that he and Seth could handle on their own. It was no longer a mishap that could be covered up.

"The supes!" he choked in the thickening smoke. "Get the supes!"

Seth was uncertain. "What are you going to do?"

"I'll – I'll take care of things here." It was pure babble, but it was enough for Seth. He raced out into the night. The rush of air from the door fed the flames, which were reaching for the roosts. The hens scattered in agitation.

Aiden was sure there were a million things he should be doing. Yet in this frantic moment, only one thought possessed him. He had to save the chickens.

The chickens didn't agree. Or at least they were so worked up by the smoke and fire that they could not be herded towards the door.

The moment was as absurd as it was awful. His parents were locked up for life; he and Meg were exiled to a prison farm, a place he had just set on fire. And what was he doing? Rampaging around a smoke-filled henhouse, windmilling his arms and screaming in an attempt to scare the chickens outside.

He burst through the door, kicking the last bird ahead of him. A horrifying sight met his eyes. The coop was an inferno, the sheets of flame bent diagonal by a strong wind. As he watched, a gust jumped the blaze to the top of the log rail fence. The ancient wood was like kindling. The fire tightrope-walked across it, advancing quickly and steadily towards—

"The barn!"

It would be next, with the cows trapped in their stalls. Aiden loathed those animals, but they couldn't be left to die. Not that way.

He threw open the door and barrelled into the manure smell. It was so dark that he moved by touch alone, pawing at stall barriers and big bodies.

"Everybody out!"

His cries had little effect on the sleeping cattle. He pounded on their sides and kicked at their legs with all his might – anything to start them ambling towards the door and safety.

Now he could see smoke curling in through the

gaps between the wallboards. The outside structure was on fire. There wasn't much time.

"Come on, you idiots! *Move!*"

There were nine cows at Sunnydale. He had to drag them out one at a time. One head-butted him into a post, one tried to bite him, and four kicked him after he had led them outside. Some gratitude.

By this time, the entire chicken coop was engulfed in a pillar of flame twenty feet high. Its collapse was spectacular, sending a fountain of sparks up into the night sky.

Aiden gawked, awestruck, as the wind scattered the thousands of airborne embers. They sailed high over the main house and then descended like a blanket to cover the wood-shingle roof. There was instant combustion.

His alarm soared to a new and more urgent level. This wasn't about chickens and cows any more. That house was full of people!

And the next thought, far more terrifying:

Meg.

The girls' dormitory was smaller than the boys', but with identical rows of bunk beds on each side of the room.

Meg was the only girl in bed, staring at the blank piece of paper that was supposed to be a letter to her mother.

What's there to say? she thought morosely. *That I hate it here? It'll only make her feel worse.*

One thing was clear. No matter how terrible Sunnydale Farm may have been, a federal penitentiary had to be a thousand times worse.

She sniffed. Smoke. Leticia was probably lighting up again. The girl must have a ten-year supply of cigarettes hidden here somewhere. The supervisors searched the place twice a week and still couldn't find anything.

She peered through the door to the adjoining TV lounge where the rest of the girls were gathered. Odd – no one was smoking. A few of them were painting their toenails. That blew Meg's mind. Convicted of robbery, assault, drug dealing and grand theft auto, they were acting like this was a gigglefest slumber party.

When she heard the yelling, she rushed to the window and threw up the blinds. Whatever was happening, it was on the other side of the building, where the animals were. But the yard looked somehow – wrong. There was an eerie reflective glow.

The northern lights? In Nebraska?

A groaning sound filled the room. The floor shuddered.

An earthquake?

And then the ceiling disintegrated, and it was raining fire.

A large chunk of burning roof tile hit the pillow inches from her head. With a cry of shock, Meg hurled herself to the floor and rolled for cover. But there was no cover. Hot sparks singed her face.

Out in the TV lounge, there were screams, followed by a mad scramble.

Breathing into her T-shirt, Meg took a quick inventory of herself. Nothing broken, nothing burning. A large chunk of roof barred the way to the lounge – the only exit. A wall of flame.

"Help me!" she screamed. "I can't get out!"

There was no response, no sound at all. They had abandoned her here.

She looked around wildly. There had to be a way out. "There's a solution for everything," Mom had always said, "if you're willing to take the time to think it through."

She yanked the top drawer out of the nightstand, dumped the contents, and raced over to the window. Swinging with all her strength, she began to hack at the glass. To her dismay, it broke but did not shatter.

It was security glass, she recalled in growing panic, with wire mesh embedded in each pane.

With reserve power she didn't know she had, she picked up the entire nightstand and flung it. It struck the window and bounced away.

She stepped back. *Can't get through the door; can't get through the window. No other exit.*

Unbelievable. She was going to die in this fire.

And all because I didn't want to paint my stupid toenails!

"Meg!"

Out of the fire itself appeared a steaming, smouldering shape, staggering directly through the burning roof tiles that blocked the door. Meg looked on in amazement as the flaming blanket was flung aside to reveal Aiden, wild-eyed and desperate.

"How did you do that?" she blurted. "Why aren't you dead?"

In answer, he ripped the blankets off two bunks and dragged her into the adjoining bathroom. He turned the shower on full blast and crammed both of them into the spray.

She stared at him. "This is safe?"

"In *The Case of the Pharaoh's Mask*—" he panted.

"Dad's *book*?" She began to beat at his chest and face with her open hands. "You got this from Dad's book? Are you crazy? The biggest fire he ever survived was a backyard barbecue!"

Aiden was too exhausted to answer, but his expression said it all. Maybe this wasn't safe, but it was infinitely safer than staying here to burn.

He draped one of the dripping blankets over her head and wrapped himself in the other one.

"Hold your breath!" he said harshly. "And whatever you do, don't stop!"

They ran, bursting through the flame-obscured doorway. Cowering under the wet wrapper, Meg couldn't see. But she knew when she was in the fire. There was extreme heat, and, most terrifying of all, a total absence of air – a baking vacuum.

And then it was over. Aiden ripped the blanket away, revealing the TV room, with the blaze miraculously behind them. "Roll!" he commanded.

She did. At that moment, she would have obeyed if he'd asked her to fly.

They pounded at each other's wet clothing, beating out any smouldering spots.

"Are you OK?" he rasped.

But Meg was listening to something else – an all-too-familiar creaking sound from above. The rest of the roof was about to cave in.

She grabbed her brother's hand. *"Run!!"* The two

of them blasted out of the building. The roar that came from behind told them the roof was collapsing in their wake. But they never looked back.

Outside was pure chaos, with the helpless supervisors squirting extinguisher foam on a fire that had already consumed everything in its path. The outbuildings were ashes. Cows, geese, chickens, and residents milled around in the confusion. Aiden got no more than fifty feet from the house before collapsing to the dirt, physically and emotionally drained.

"It's OK," Meg soothed. "We made it."

"How can it be OK? Look around you!"

Meg shrugged. "What do we care if their jail burns down?"

"But it's all my fault!"

Meg goggled. "You torched the farm?"

Aiden gasped out the story of the mishap with the kerosene lamp. "I could have put it out! I was *going* to – I just waited a few seconds! But by then it was too late. The supes are going to kill me!"

Meg drew him to his feet and led him further away from the remains of the building. "The supes are never going to see you again," she said. "We can be a long way from here by sunrise."

Aiden was horrified. "You mean take off? Don't you think we're in enough trouble already?"

"We're the only ones who *aren't* in trouble!" she argued. "They have no real right to keep us here. Besides, there is no 'here' any more."

Aiden was racked with guilt. "Aren't you listening to me? I have to turn myself in. Somebody could be dead in that fire. It was almost *you*."

"The girls all got out," she reasoned, "and the boys had plenty of warning." She took hold of him by the shoulders. "Listen, bro. You just saved my life. Now I'm going to save yours. Let's blow this Popsicle stand."

His eyes were hopeless. "We'll never make it."

"The supes have their hands full," she insisted. "You think we'll be the only ones missing when the ashes cool? Besides, when they investigate, they'll hear that the roof fell on me, and you were in a barbecued chicken coop. Maybe they'll think we're dead."

"Even if we can get away," Aiden argued back, "we're in the middle of nowhere. We have no place to go, no money. You're in your pyjamas. I'm in a jumpsuit that might as well have a sign that says JAILBIRD."

"This is what we've been praying for – a chance to get out of here, to help Mom and Dad! I don't know how we'll do it, but we definitely can't if we're locked away." She played her trump card. "This place is dust. God knows where they'll send us next. We might not even be together. This is a gift, Aiden. Say thank you and fly."

Over Meg's shoulder, Aiden saw the east wall of the main house collapse in a cascade of smoke and embers.

Whatever lay ahead, this chapter of their lives was over.

They sprinted for the cornfield.

We're fugitives.

The thought bounced off the walls of Aiden's brain as he and his sister tramped through fields that seemed to have no end. The harvest moon and a billion stars lit their way for a while. But when the clouds rolled in, the prairie night wrapped them in velvet black. Soon their faces were scratched from the tall cornstalks.

One advantage of the zero visibility was that Aiden had finally stopped glancing over his shoulder, expecting to find Ray and the other supervisors bearing down on them. He wasn't any less scared, but why look when there was no chance of seeing anything anyway?

"This can't still be our cornfield," Meg complained. "We've been walking for ages."

"This is Nebraska," Aiden reminded her. "You can cross the whole state without leaving cornfields."

In three hours they had not yet come to a single road. But they knew one was not far away. They could hear distant sirens as emergency vehicles converged on Sunnydale Farm. Aiden pictured a fire truck roaring up to the facility to find every man-made structure already gone.

"My feet are killing me," groaned Meg. "I think my slippers disintegrated an hour ago."

Aiden was shocked. Because he was wearing work boots, he'd assumed that Meg was, too. But no, she had on the thin slippers that were issued to the residents for use in the main house – flimsy, barely socks.

"We can't stop," he told her. "Want to wear my boots for a while?"

"Those clodhoppers? I'd be crippled in an hour."

And they pushed on.

They reached their first road after midnight and trudged along the soft shoulder. Where they were headed was anybody's guess. At this point, the only important direction was *away*.

It was easier going, but the appearance of every set of headlights had them diving into the corn. For all they knew, word of the fire had spread via the media, and the entire county was searching for escapees from Sunnydale.

Fugitives have no friends.

But they couldn't stay hidden for ever. Especially not in the daylight. Come sunrise, they had to find a way to blend in, to look normal.

"We need clothes," Aiden decided.

"No problem," Meg said sarcastically. "I'll weave a new wardrobe out of some of this corn silk."

"I'm serious. We need to be able to walk around without attracting attention. We can't look like we just broke out of jail."

"It's no big mystery, bro. There are no stores, and even if there were, we have no money. Whatever we get, we have to steal."

Aiden made a face in the darkness. She was right, of course. She usually was. But the idea of stealing made him feel unclean. At least before, he and Meg hadn't belonged in the juvenile corrections system.

If this is what it takes to survive as fugitives, pretty soon our rap sheets will be twice as long as anybody else's.

As the adrenalin of their escape wore off, weariness set in. There were times that Aiden was pretty sure he was asleep on his feet, awakened only by the fresh twist of a leg cramp or the mild sting of yet another mosquito bite. At one point, Meg almost wandered out into the middle of the road, and

33

Aiden had to grab her and steer her back on course.

Not that there were cars any more. His watch told him it was after three. Even the distant sirens had stopped by this time. Either that or they were now out of range. Only the chirping of locusts and crickets proved to Aiden that a world existed out there in the darkness. It was a tiny comfort to know that he and Meg weren't completely alone in the universe. In this spot, at this moment, it sure felt that way.

Five a.m. – twenty-four hours since they'd last slept. God, Meg looked tired!

Then it hit him. *I can see her.* Sunrise wouldn't be for another hour or more, but after a night submerged in black ink, even the faintest pre-dawn glow brought the world into sharp focus.

Her voice startled him. "A house." He would have bet all the money he didn't have that she'd been sleepwalking.

Then he spotted it, too – a small wood-frame farmhouse with attached shed and a large modern barn in the back. The windows were dark, and – this was the kind of coincidence that always happened in Dad's detective novels – there was a carousel hung with clothes just outside the shed.

"Jackpot!" breathed Meg.

They approached cautiously. It was still mostly

dark. But farmers were notoriously early risers. It would be a tragedy to get caught clothes-napping after making it so far.

Meg whispered a logical concern. "What if nothing fits?"

"It's still better than burned pyjamas and a jail-bird suit." Her brother pulled down a pair of khakis and a T-shirt.

Meg scowled at the label on her own selection. "Fatso! Hey, can you reach those shorts?"

The dog came out of nowhere, an oversize German shepherd in full flight. Against the backdrop of stillness, the barking was like the roar of carpet bombing exploding all around them.

The Falconers dropped the clothes and ran. The animal bounded after them, and Aiden realized with a sinking heart that there was no way they could escape. Two kids, exhausted and sleep deprived, didn't stand a chance against a full-speed attack dog.

As they scrambled around the laundry carousel, Meg reached up and yanked on a large white sheet. It billowed down, engulfing the leaping dog. The shepherd yelped and hit the ground, wrapping itself in linen.

It was all the time Aiden and Meg needed. They

35

raced into the barn and clambered up the ladder to the loft. Through a small window, they could see the white sheet jerking around like a spastic ghost as the dog struggled to free itself.

"It'll come after us," quavered Meg.

"Shhh. I don't think it can get up the ladder."

Crouched amid the bales of hay, Aiden was aware of an all-too-familiar smell. He looked down into the barn. Cows. Was there no escaping them?

"Someone's coming!" Meg hissed.

Sure enough, a light was shining in the house. Then the porch lamp came on.

The Falconers threw themselves flat to the floor of the loft and prayed.

A woman's angry voice called, "Fool dog! Are you into my laundry again?"

The animal did everything but talk. In the chorus of barking, Aiden could almost hear it: *Call the police! There are two escaped convicts hiding in our hayloft!*

But all the woman could see was her soiled sheet. "Bad dog! And stay away from that barn. You *don't* rile up the cows before milking. What's gotten into you?"

Aiden sneaked a look. The woman had gone back inside. A second later, the chastised shepherd slunk into the barn. Parking itself at the bottom rung of the ladder, it glared up at the loft, sniffing and growling.

"Now what?" whispered Meg.

Aiden wasn't sure. How long would the dog wait there for them? Hours? Days? Mom and Dad had travelled a lot on the lecture circuit, so the Falconers had never had a pet. How patient could man's best friend be? And how long before the people who lived here figured out that the shepherd was trying to tell them something?

Aiden would not have believed it was possible to sleep in this situation. But the next thing he knew, it was full daylight, and Meg was flaked out in the straw beside him, dead to the world.

He gave her shoulder a gentle shake. "Meg—"

She started. "I'm awake!"

"Shhh!"

There was a mechanical hum coming from the barn below, and the occasional clanking noise. Milking machines.

Aiden risked a look down the ladder. A chorus of angry barking rose to greet him.

"Get out of here, Sparky!" snapped a man's voice. "Every time you chase a rat up that ladder, we have to put up with your infernal racket!"

The two rats in the loft looked at each other hopelessly. How were they ever going to get out of there?

At last the milking was over, and the cows were taken out to pasture. Sparky never moved a muscle. He sat like a sentry, practically hugging the base of the ladder.

"We're going to have to run for it," whispered Meg.

"We wouldn't stand a chance."

It was high noon before the farmer, his wife and three children piled into a huge SUV parked in the driveway.

"Sparky! Where is that dog?"

The eldest son ran to the barn, grabbed Sparky by the collar, and hauled him away to the car.

The Falconers did not allow themselves to breathe until the sound of the motor had faded into the distance.

They scampered down the ladder and out of the barn.

"It's a good omen," Meg decided. "It means we're lucky."

Of all the words that described their situation, "lucky" was the one Aiden would have picked last.

Back at the carousel, they selected clothes at their leisure. Aiden's khakis were loose, but a tackle harness made a suitable belt. The items Meg selected fit perfectly. There was even an old pair of sneakers that cradled her cut and bruised feet as if custom-made.

She looked hopefully at her brother. "I'm starving."

"No way," he said firmly. "For all we know, they've got a burglar alarm in that house. Or an old grandmother."

"Or another dog," she agreed, chastened. "But Aiden – look!"

Hanging on wall hooks were three well-used mountain bikes.

"We don't need them," Aiden said stubbornly. "Everybody's been treating us like criminals. Let's prove them wrong."

"They're speed. And the faster we get away from here, the safer we'll be." Meg could see she was getting through to him, and hurried on. "Besides, we're only *borrowing* them. We'll just ride to the nearest town, somewhere we can get on a train or bus."

"Yeah, but a train or a bus to *where*?" Aiden voiced the concern that had been eating him up inside since they'd first turned their backs on the burning wreckage of Sunnydale. "Where is this mystery destination of ours?"

"Florida," Meg replied readily. "That's where Mom and Dad are."

A wave of tenderness washed over him. His little sister had so much spirit. She was bent down by these past months but never broken.

"To do what?" he asked gently. "To bust them out of jail? You're talking about federal prisons, Meg. You can't knock them out with a kerosene lamp. Besides, that's the first place they'll look for us."

Her expression grew stormy. "Well, what's *your* plan, besides shooting holes in mine? Our parents are in jail because we can't get our act together to get them out!"

Aiden knew he had to reach her — really reach her — and right now. "There's nothing I wouldn't give for the four of us to be together as a family again. But to say that Mom and Dad are where they are because of us — you'll drive yourself crazy thinking that way. This is *not* within our power to change. Our parents are locked up because Frank Lindenauer wouldn't come forward to admit they worked for the CIA. That's it."

"Well, then, that's what we have to do," she said simply. "We'll find Frank Lindenauer."

Her brother stared at her. He did not have the heart to drag her back to cruel reality again. To explain that if teams of lawyers and private investigators couldn't find Lindenauer, what chance did two kids on the run have? She would have to face it sooner or later, but not today. Today the poor kid had to win at something.

"We'll take the bikes," he conceded.

After drinking deeply at the garden hose and inhaling a few not-quite-ripe peaches from the tree in the front yard, the Falconers returned to the road, this time on wheels.

Once he was riding down the two-lane highway, Aiden's spirits improved. Being on a bike again just seemed so – normal. It was something from his regular life, not this improbable nightmare that had replaced it. The wind in his hair felt great.

Meg had to feel it, too. *At eleven years old*, Aiden thought, *this is what she should be doing, not fleeing for her life*. Meg was too young to really remember the summer the Falconers had vacationed with "Uncle Frank" – the only time Aiden remembered meeting Frank Lindenauer.

It was amazing. After all the years the Falconers had known the man – even before they knew of his CIA connection – they didn't have a single photograph of him, or a single document with his name on it. Nothing that would prove his existence.

Yet Aiden recalled that vacation vividly. He'd been six, and Meg not quite two. The memories of the house were the clearest – a pretty white cottage with red shutters, on the Vermont side of Lake Champlain. The Falconers had gone back there for several summers after that. Enough years that Aiden had established his own secret hiding place behind a loose piece of panelling in his tiny bedroom. It made him blush to think of what passed for treasure in those days – bottle caps, rocks, Cracker Jack prizes, and a handful of pictures from his sixth birthday present, a little box camera. He could almost see the array of dumb family photos: Mom and Dad clowning around, Meg in her stroller, Uncle Frank and his girlfriend in lounge chairs—

Without warning, Aiden's bike veered off the shoulder and into the ditch, dumping him unceremoniously in the tall grass. He lay there, stunned, as Meg leaped off her own bicycle and rushed to his side.

"Aiden! What happened?"

He accepted her proffered hand and hauled himself to his feet. "I –" It hardly seemed possible after everything that had happened – the investigation, the defence, the trial. And yet it was staring him right in the face. "I think I've got a picture of Frank Lindenauer!"

Breathlessly, he explained to Meg about the summer-house in Vermont.

She was furious. "Why didn't you remember that when it was important? When the trial was going on?"

"It wouldn't have made the difference between guilty and innocent," Aiden reasoned. "It's just a picture of a guy sitting by the pool."

"So what good is it to us now?" asked Meg, deflated.

"Maybe none. But it's somewhere to start. It's our only clue." He looked hopeful. "A name can be faked, but you can't fake a face. If the picture's still there, we have someone to look for."

All at once, Meg was energized again. "Well, what are we waiting for?"

Aiden was actually laughing as he stood up and righted his bike on the pavement. There was something contagious about his sister's enthusiasm, but he had to bring her back to earth. "It's not as easy as you think, Meg. We haven't been there in years. I don't have an address."

She was unperturbed. "Vermont. East."

By the crazy logic of the fix they were in, it almost made sense. To stay here meant capture. They had to go somewhere.

Why not Vermont?

Agent Emmanuel Harris of the FBI took a sip of coffee and nearly sprayed it all over his desk. How was his lame-brain assistant ever going to make it as an investigator if she couldn't even remember that her boss took his coffee black? Black meant black — no milk, no powdered stuff, no sugar, no Nutra-Sweet. Harris was a tolerant man, but that didn't extend to coffee.

He was about to unleash his famous sarcasm, his fist hovering over the intercom button, when he spied the item on his computer screen. The Bureau provided its agents with real-time updates on all law-enforcement stories around the world. It was just a few lines — barely a paragraph. But the words jumped out at him — *Juvenile Corrections*.

GIBBON, NEBRASKA: A suspicious fire last night destroyed Sunnydale Farm, an alternative mini-mum-security detention facility run by the Department of Juvenile Corrections. No injuries have been reported, but seventeen of thirty inmates are still at large and possibly dangerous. . .

"Not my problem," he said aloud, but made no move to scroll down from the report.

They were in the juvenile system somewhere. That was where they'd been bounced after the foster homes hadn't worked out.

Silly, he told himself. There were tens of thousands of teens in hundreds of facilities around the country. This was one little farm. The chance they were involved was less than slim. And yet. . .

He found himself dialling the number of the Department of Juvenile Corrections in Washington, DC. There was the usual runaround before Harris found himself on the phone with Deputy Director Adler.

"I heard you had a little trouble at Sunnydale Farm in Nebraska last night. Any idea if Aiden and Meg Falconer are among the missing?"

There was a long pause on the line. Then, "I can check the list. Give me the spelling of their last name."

46

With effort, Harris uncrossed his long legs and crossed them in the other direction. He was six foot seven, and the FBI didn't seem to have a desk large enough to accommodate him. "Falconer. As in the children of John and Louise Falconer."

"Oh!" The deputy director sounded ruffled. "*Those* Falconers. Well — uh — I'll have to look into. . ."

Harris wasn't listening any longer. The young Falconers' identity was probably under the highest level of secrecy. But he could hear it in Adler's voice. Something was up with those kids. And the department didn't want to admit it.

Adler was still hemming and hawing. ". . .so if you'll leave your number, I'll get back to you when I have more information." Then he added, "What's the big interest in these two, anyway?"

Harris let out his breath and realized he'd been holding it.

"I'm the one who put their parents away for life."

It wasn't a town exactly, or even a village. It was more a cluster of modest homes dotted around a gas station with a mini-mart.

Aiden and Meg left the road and struggled with their bikes over uneven ground and through dense underbrush. They were still too close to Sunnydale to risk being seen by the local population.

But as they circled around the back of the ramshackle garage, Aiden had a change of heart.

"I think we have to go in there," he murmured, gesturing to the mini-mart.

Meg was nervous. "Shouldn't we stay out of sight?"

"As much as we can," he agreed. "But look." He pointed to the flyspecked window at the rear of the store. Inside, tacked to the wall behind the cash register, was a large map. "It'll tell us where the towns are around here. We'll never get anywhere if we can't find a place with some transportation."

They stashed their bikes in an undergrowth of honeysuckle and crept towards the gas station, staying low in the tall grass. With Aiden in the lead, they came around the corner of the building and surveyed the terrain.

The mini-mart was empty. At the pumps stood a tall, gangly teenager in oil-spattered coveralls, filling up a Ford pickup and making small talk with the driver. His back was to them.

Aiden decided to chance it. Pulling Meg by the hand, he darted across the blacktop and eased open the door of the mini-mart. He was congratulating himself on their stealth when the bell sounded.

It was only a little ringer attached to the door. But to the two fugitives, it might as well have been a bomb blast. Aiden jumped, and Meg let out a yelp of shock.

The gas attendant looked over, and the Falconers rushed inside, faces averted.

From the grease pit adjoining the store, a voice called, "Be with you folks in a few minutes." Through the glass, they could see light coming from beneath an old Chevy.

"No hurry," said Aiden in a shaky voice. The two went straight to the map.

They were in a place called Buffalo County, Nebraska.

"No wonder they didn't need bars to keep us at Sunnydale," Meg whispered. "Where was there to go?"

"Shhh," Aiden cautioned. "Right there." His finger traced a single line marked with short crossbars. It traversed the county from east to west. "Railway tracks," he told her. "And not too far from here. If we can find those tracks, all we have to do is follow them until we come to a station. Probably in – " he pointed – "Gibbon."

"Where's that from here?" asked Meg.

"South. We're headed east. That means we just

have to find somewhere to make a right turn and keep on going until we hit the tracks."

Meg nodded. "Let's get moving."

The country-western music coming from the radio in the grease pit was replaced by an announcer's voice. *"It's eighty degrees in Omaha, eighty-two in Lincoln and seventy-six in Scott's Bluff. In news around the state, police and juvenile authorities continue to search south-central Nebraska, rounding up the runaways from the Sunnydale Juvenile Detention Centre."*

Aiden froze with his hand on the doorknob.

"The facility burned to the ground under mysterious circumstances last night. No one was injured, but eleven of thirty young offenders are still unaccounted for.

"In national news. . ."

A sharp finger in the ribs brought Aiden back to life.

"Come *on*!" hissed Meg.

Aiden threw open the door. There, wiping his hands on a dirty rag, stood a burly middle-aged man with a smudged face under a three-day growth of beard.

His eyes narrowed at the sight of them. "Never seen you kids around here before."

Aiden was too devastated for speech. They had finally found a purpose – were heading towards something. They had a plan, no matter how flimsy. And it was all coming to an end because the local news in Nowheresville, Nebraska, came on at the wrong time.

Meg stepped around him and gave the man a dazzling smile with full teeth and dimples. "You can say that again, mister. We are *so* lost!"

He looked unconvinced. "Where are you heading?"

"We're staying at our uncle's place. He's got a pig farm outside Kearney. And – no offence, I'm sure it's a great place – but it stinks to high heaven. I mean, we were *choking*! So we got on our bikes and rode out. Aunt Cassie is going to kill us."

He studied her face. "That would be Cassie Whipple out at the old Ackerman property?"

Aiden held his breath and tried to communicate with his sister by telepathy: *It's a trap!*

He needn't have worried. Meg did not rise to the bait. "No. Cassie Ferguson. Aunt Cassie and Uncle Don. So anyway, we came in to check your map."

"So you know you kids are way off course. Kearney's twenty miles west of here."

"Yeah, thanks," said Meg. "Come on, bro, we'd better hit the road."

They breezed past him and walked quickly across

the blacktop, feeling the man's eyes – and the gas jockey's, too – burning into the backs of their heads. The instant they were around the side of the building, they broke into a full sprint to where they'd left the bikes.

A moment later they were speeding off down the road towards Kearney.

"Isn't this the wrong way?" called Meg.

"It's the right way to Aunt Cassie's house," Aiden shot back sarcastically. "We can't let that guy catch us riding east."

The last thing they saw before the gas station fell out of sight behind them was the big greasy mechanic dialling the mini-mart's phone.

"Aw, man, he's calling the cops!" Aiden groaned.

"Maybe he's calling his girlfriend," Meg suggested. "Or his mother."

"We've got to get off this road!" Even as he spoke the words, his heart was sinking. One thing they'd learned from the ride so far: intersections were few and far between in this part of Nebraska.

They pedalled on west, unable to turn back. Aiden kept his eyes peeled for a way south – a dirt road, a cow path, anything that would get them away from here. The authorities were on the way. He had no doubt of that.

"Maybe we should ditch the bikes and cross these fields on foot," Meg suggested.

"We're too far out in the middle of nowhere. Gibbon is still miles away."

Going in the wrong direction, even when it was necessary, was driving Aiden crazy. *Pretty soon we'll pass the farm where we stole these bikes,* he thought miserably. *Then it's only a hop, skip and jump back to Sunnydale.*

His ears strained to detect the faint whine of sirens. At any moment he expected a line of cop cars to explode from behind a stand of corn. The tension welled up inside him to the point where he almost wanted to get caught, just so the awful uncertainty would be over.

"Look!" cried Meg.

A road – a narrow, dusty two-lane thoroughfare, completely identical to the route they were on. But this one headed south.

They wheeled around the corner with new energy. Just the thought that every turn of the pedals was taking them closer to where they needed to be lent Aiden's feet wings. Meg must have felt it, too, because she was matching him rpm for rpm. In no time at all, they had covered so much ground that they could no longer see the turn-off behind them.

He caught a glimpse of his sister riding alongside him. Her face was glowing with effort and purpose. She flashed him a thumbs-up and called, "Vermont!"

He tried to look encouraging. Vermont, maybe. But Aiden would have settled for the heck away from here.

He pictured the mini-mart map in his mind, trying to estimate the distance to the train tracks. It was hard to translate inches on the poster into miles of lush farmland. But surely another hour or two would get them there.

When the horn sounded, it was a hammer blow to the heart. The pickup truck was practically beside them, its driver gesturing for them to stop.

Aiden pedalled harder, even as he knew that two kids on bikes couldn't outrun a motor vehicle. Stupid of them to get so wrapped up in the glory of their escape that they failed to notice a truck until it was upon them.

The driver rolled down his window. "I just want to talk!" he called.

"Keep going!" Meg screamed at her brother.

All at once, the pickup lurched ahead of them and screeched to a halt, blocking their way.

7

Both Falconers leaped off their bikes to avoid a painful collision.

Meg hit the ground running, but Aiden was pitched into the ditch.

The driver jumped out of his truck. "Hey!"

As Aiden struggled to climb the embankment, he suddenly recognized their pursuer. It was the teenage attendant from the gas station.

"What do you want from us?" Aiden demanded, steeling himself to fight for their freedom.

"You're from Sunnydale, right? The kids who ran away?"

"So what?" Aiden shot back.

"I was there. When I was fifteen. I did a year on that farm."

Meg turned around. "There's no such place any more."

The teenager grinned. "No tears from this graduate."

"Is that what this is about?" asked Aiden. "An alumni meeting? We're in kind of a hurry."

The attendant turned serious. "You're in a *big* hurry. Jimmy – my boss – ratted you out. You've got to ditch those bikes. I'll drop them up north a ways – throw the cops off the scent."

The look that passed between Aiden and Meg spoke volumes. Ever since their parents' arrest, they had been mistreated, lied to, jerked around, ignored and neglected. Worse, they had been treated as if they were guilty of some unspecified vile crime. It had never occurred to them that anyone might try to help them.

"Thanks for the heads-up," Aiden said finally. "Can you tell us how far the railway tracks are?"

"Three, maybe four miles. But it's not safe on the road. Cut through the fields, keep low. And take these." He reached into the cab of the pickup and pulled out two shrink-wrapped submarine sandwiches from the mini-mart.

"We have no money," Aiden said stiffly.

The gas jockey smiled. "Jimmy's food tastes like wet newspaper. Trust me – you're paying exactly what it's worth." He loaded the first of the bikes into the truck's flatbed. "Now, take off."

*

56

Meg hated ham and cheese. But her mini-mart sandwich tasted like it had been prepared by a gourmet chef. She finished it down to the last crumb, then licked at bits of mustard on her fingers.

She turned a jaundiced eye on her brother, trudging beside her through the wheat field. Aiden still had three-quarters of his sandwich left. He was nibbling slowly, savouring every morsel, making it last.

"You're doing that on purpose," she said irritably.

"Doing what?"

"Waving that lousy sandwich in my face when you know I haven't got one."

"You had one. You ate it."

"Like a normal person," she insisted. "I didn't turn it into a three-day picnic."

"Do you want a piece?" he offered.

"No. It's yours."

"Well, then, let me eat it," he mumbled, mouth full. "My way."

But after a few more bites, he took the wad of clear plastic from his pocket, carefully unfolded it, and rewrapped the remaining half sandwich.

"Now what are you doing?" Meg demanded.

"Saving it for later. Who knows when our next meal will be."

She stormed ahead, putting her brother and his annoying habits out of her sight. Aiden always had to have a plan, even for something as stupid as a ham sandwich. What could you expect from a kid who used to sort his Halloween candy into alphabetical order and would still be eating the Zagnuts in April? It was almost as if his personality had been custom-crafted to get on Meg's nerves.

Hey, she reminded herself sharply, *he didn't get on your nerves when he busted through smoke and flames to rescue you.*

But even then Aiden had needed an instruction manual – the how-to he'd taken from one of Dad's cheese-ball detective novels. How was a guy like that going to get all the way from a wheat field in Nebraska to a place in Vermont he barely even remembered, with no money and no plan?

The challenge that lay ahead simply could not be met by a person like Aiden. This called for someone who could think on her feet and fly by the seat of her pants.

Someone like Meg.

It's my job to get us through this. I have to be sharp, on my toes. I can't let anything get past me—

"Meg!"

She looked back and realized instantly that between her and Aiden was a railway track. She had actually walked right over it and missed it.

They made a left turn and walked along the line of the track. Somewhere on this shiny double rail to infinity lay the station at Gibbon, where two fugitive kids could hop a freight east.

Gibbon. It was still miles away. Ten? Twenty? Fifty?

Every time she pictured the mini-mart map, the dot that was Gibbon had somehow slithered further away from them.

She swallowed her pride. "Hey, bro, how about we crack open that half sandwich?"

"We should probably wait," he warned, but finally gave in.

This time the food wasn't half as satisfying in her mouth, the ham too salty, the bread stale. Of course they should have held out longer. Why was Aiden always right?

She cast him a resentful look, and her eye was caught by a speck over his shoulder — a moving speck.

He was instantly alert to her distress. "What?"

She pointed. "I'm being paranoid, right? There are millions of reasons for a helicopter to be up there."

"Sure," Aiden said uncertainly, and couldn't name one. "But just in case —" He did a three-sixty. Nothing but acre after acre of golden wheat. Not a shrub, not a rock. Zero cover.

Eleven of us unaccounted for in a big open state. . . Meg felt the panic rising in her throat. Of course the juvenile authorities would search by air! At ground level, you could disappear into the Nebraska fields. But not when you were being hunted from above.

Aiden grabbed her arm and began running alongside the rails.

"Don't you think we have a better chance just lying in the wheat?" she cried. But then she saw it, too. About a quarter mile ahead, the tracks crossed a river via a narrow trestle bridge. If they could make it before the chopper got close enough to spot them—

They flew, with all the misery and horror of the past months acting as their booster rockets.

Meg risked a glance over her shoulder. The features of the helicopter were fully visible now. It was a bubble top, moving in a sweeping motion back and forth over the fields — a classic search pattern. She was sure she would have heard the clatter of the rotors except for the pounding of her own heart in her ears.

Their heavy footfalls made a gonging sound as the Falconers pounded on to the metal of the bridge.

Aiden swung a leg up to straddle the railing. "Get underneath!" he rasped. "Fast!"

Meg didn't have to be told twice.

They eased themselves over the side and climbed spiderlike along the support girders until they were well hidden by the top of the bridge. Gasping, they hung there, directly below the midpoint of the span.

"Do you think they saw us?" said Meg, quavering.

"We'll know soon enough."

They listened for several minutes. The sound of the chopper swelled and faded as it continued the track lines of its search. A good sign – it meant the crew hadn't noticed anything out of the ordinary.

Meg felt the muscles in her arms cramping up as she attempted to wiggle herself into a more comfortable position in the crook of two girders.

All at once, she detected a different sensation – a superfast vibration that seemed to permeate her entire body.

She looked over at her brother. "Do you feel like you're buzzing all over?"

The expression on his face was pure agony. "Hang on, Meg, and hang on tight! There's a train coming!"

Meg could hear it now, the great lumbering locomotive, the rumble of many hundreds of wheels, and the screech of brakes as the engineer slowed down to take the bridge. The roar drowned out the sound of the helicopter.

And it was growing louder. The vibration grew so intense that Meg was positive her teeth were jarring loose.

The train hurtled out on to the steel span above them. The noise was unimaginable – the squeal of metal on metal far louder than any jet engine. It was as if the bridge itself went into convulsions, shaking the Falconers like rag dolls in the mouth of an angry terrier.

Robbed of all but the barest consciousness, Meg shut her eyes and squeezed the girder. A single thought played like a tune through her agony: *Mom and Dad will never find out what happened to us. . .*

The wild vibration acted like Novocain on her body. Numbness set in; she could not feel the girder. Her eyes blinked open, and she realized in horror that it was no longer there.

She was falling.

Then she was in the cool water, shocked to awareness and choking. The compulsion to swim for air was automatic. She broke the surface just in time to see a huge cannonball splash beside her. A second later, her brother bobbed up. The caboose cleared the bridge, and the noise began to fade as the train moved off.

"Are you OK?" Aiden spluttered.

She nodded. "The chopper?"

Treading water, they both peered up from their position in the shadow of the bridge. The helicopter was gone. The crisis was over as quickly as it had come upon them.

Typically, Aiden was agonizing over their close call, shivering and reliving every moment of the ordeal.

Leave it to him, Meg thought, *to obsess over something that didn't happen.*

"Aiden, we made it!" she interrupted. "What's the big deal?"

*

The big deal turned out to be this: they now had to finish their long walk to Gibbon in drenched discomfort.

The day was warm and sunny, but dusk was at hand, and clouds of mosquitoes rose from the fields, looking to light on any damp surface. The T-shirts dried after an hour or so, but the trousers stayed soggy, clinging, chafing. The shoes didn't dry at all, squishing and oozing with every step.

The night was hideous. Aiden stumbled along the tracks, his arms windmilling as he slapped at the dozens of mosquitoes attacking his body.

"Do you have to do that?" Meg muttered into the deepening darkness. "They're mosquitoes, bro, not piranhas."

"That's easy for you to say. They're not eating you alive. I've got fair skin, and the water attracts them, you know."

She was unmoved. "If you didn't want to get wet, you shouldn't have fallen off that bridge."

"I didn't fall off," he retorted, killing three bugs with one slap. "I jumped off – to rescue you."

Meg bit her lip. Who was she crabbing at? The only person who cared what happened to her.

Soon it was every bit as dark as it had been the night before – that suffocating unbroken blackness that made them feel they were the only two people left in the world. At least tonight they had the tracks to keep them on their course.

Just before midnight, another train came by, this one a westbound freight. Hiding amid the wheat, Aiden noticed in the passing glow of its single headlight that both his arms were covered in raised welts. The word "itch" didn't do justice to the feeling.

But the real enemy was not the mosquitoes, nor the chafed skin, nor aching feet. Lack of sleep was catching up with the Falconers. They had dozed only a couple of hours in the hayloft. The rest of the time, they had been not only awake but on the run, operating at top awareness and energy.

If we can't get a few hours' rest, something awful's going to happen, Aiden thought numbly. But how could they stop now? Miserable as it was, darkness was the best time for them to travel out in the open like this. *If we could only make it to Gibbon and stow away on a freight train. Then we could get some sleep.*

They saw their first electric light at about two a.m., a bare bulb outside a barn that housed a fertilizer wholesaler. Other signs of civilization flickered ahead.

"Is this the town?" Meg asked in dismay.

"Probably just the outskirts," he told her. "There's

supposed to be a train station around here somewhere."

As they plodded on, the lights became more plen-
tiful, and houses and low buildings appeared.

At last, there it was – a small, low, shedlike structure next to a level street crossing. On the side, a single lamp lit a one-word sign: GIBBON.

According to the schedule posted on the bulletin
board, the first eastbound train of the day would
stop here at 4.48 a.m.

"It's perfect," said Aiden. "It'll still be dark, with
not too many people around. We can sneak into a
boxcar without anybody seeing us."

"That's two hours from now," Meg calculated.
"Let's find someplace to grab a nap in the mean-
time."

"No naps!" Aiden was adamant. "If we fall asleep
now, a train wouldn't wake us unless it was running
over our heads! We can't let the sun rise on us in this
town. This is the first station east of Sunnydale."

"Well, can we at least see if we can get into the
station? I'd give anything for a real bathroom."

The lock turned out to be broken, and they
slipped inside with no trouble.

Just enough light was coming in through the high
windows for them to make out wooden benches and

a small ticket and information kiosk.

By feeling her way along the wall, Meg located the ladies' room.

"No lights," Aiden reminded her. He sat down on a bench. No sooner was he settled on to the seat than his eyelids began to droop. He stood up quickly. *Great,* he thought. *Now I can't even trust myself to relax for a minute.*

There was a rustling sound behind him. He sat down sharply, no longer in danger of dozing. *Stay cool,* he told himself. *It's probably just a stray cat or a squirrel.*

Then it came again, and this time he was positive he heard a footstep. Somebody was in there! His imagination swelled with visions of muggers, murderers and gangsters. But even if it was merely a homeless guy looking for a place to crash, that was almost as bad. He and Meg could not be seen by *anybody*.

Avoiding sudden moves, Aiden shuffled over to the ladies' room and opened the door partway. "Hurry up," he whispered softly.

"Huh?" said Meg over the sound of running water in the sink.

"Let's go, Meg," he hissed. "Now!"

At the sound of her approach, he grabbed her

wrist and began hauling her to the exit. There was the pounding of running feet, and the Falconers ran, too.

Aiden was reaching for the knob when the other figure slammed into him, driving him back into his sister. The three tumbled to the floor. A split second later, the intruder leaped on top of Aiden, pinning him. Aiden felt metal, cold and sharp, pressed against his throat. A weapon.

A rush of terror shot through him, and he found himself looking up through wide eyes at the face of—

"*Miguel?*"

"*Eagledink?*"

Meg's foot snapped out of the darkness and connected with the side of Miguel's head. The blow knocked him off Aiden and into the station door. In a lightning-fast move, he was on his feet again, brandishing a sharpened screwdriver at Meg.

Aiden jumped in between them. "It's only my sister! She didn't know it was you!"

The dark-haired boy lowered the weapon. "Little sis packs a wallop!" He squinted in the darkness from face to face. "I'm impressed, Eagledink. I thought a wimp like you would be back at Sunnydale, helping the supes clean up the mess."

"That shows what *you* know!" Meg said belliger-ently.

Miguel nodded. "I was worried. After what I said that time about the farm being a firetrap, I figured you'd be diming me as the pyro."

"I know you didn't do it," Aiden muttered, tight-lipped.

"Yeah? How?" Miguel's mouth dropped open. "Eagledink – *you*? I was just bluffing! You must be bugging to really try it!"

"It was an accident," Aiden insisted.

"However it happened," Meg put in, "we're not going back there."

"Amen to that," Miguel agreed fervently. "Hope this train's going to Jersey. The sooner I get to my brother's crib, the better. Where are you guys headed?"

"Delaware," said Aiden, at the same time as Meg said, "Virginia."

"Oooh, you don't trust me." Miguel grinned, tak-ing mock offence. "Who can I tell without giving *myself* up? Like I care where you losers go. Hey, anybody hungry?"

"You've got food?" Meg asked anxiously.

Miguel pointed to a dark shape beside the information kiosk. "Candy machine."

"We don't have any money," said Aiden.

"My treat." Miguel jammed the screwdriver into the tool slot of the coin box and prised open the metal plate. Quarters cascaded on to the floor.

Aiden and Meg exchanged a look. They weren't thieves. Their honesty was what separated them from people like Miguel.

He read their minds. "You've got a lot of integrity for arsonists," he commented, investing some of his ill-gotten gains in a Snickers. "Remember, nobody's going to give you a reward for not robbing this machine."

Aiden hesitated. Was he crazy to think of himself and Meg as being better than Miguel? The three of them were fugitives, wanted by the law. And they were all guilty of stealing. The civilian clothes on their backs proved that. What was to be gained by denying themselves a couple of Mars bars? He and Meg were in a desperate situation. The odds against reaching Vermont had to be astronomical. It made no sense to tip them further. Why refuse nourishment just to preserve the fine line between themselves and Miguel? It probably didn't exist anyway.

"Why not?" he said with a twisted smile.

Meg had already scooped up a handful of coins and was stuffing them into the machine.

Miguel watched in amusement. "*That's* the spirit. It's a long way to Delaware. Or Virginia."

The four forty-eight pulled into Gibbon station a few minutes early. Truck farmers were spread along the road, their bushel baskets ready for loading on to the boxcars. The train crew was in position to open up cars five and six in the powerful spotlights of the work area. To anyone inside that brighter-than-day zone, this train had no engine, nor any caboose. The lights were blinding, the night around them inky-black.

Far behind the loading area, nearly a quarter of a mile to the rear, three shadowy figures slipped out of the underbrush and stole over to car forty-one, the third last on the long freight.

A hand reached up, released the latch, and slid the heavy metal door slightly open. An athletic silhouette hoisted itself up and inside, then bent down to assist two companions.

When the corrugated metal was pulled shut

again, it left no sign that anyone had ever been there.

The interior was pitch-black, darker even than the Nebraska night, and soundless, except for the ragged breathing of the three runaways.

Suddenly, a match blazed, illuminating all three of their faces. Miguel shone this temporary light into the four corners of the car. It was empty except for a few tattered sheets of newsprint and a single large crate pushed up against the front wall.

"Looks like we got the presidential suite," he said cheerfully.

"Let's just hope we don't get fleas," was Meg's comment.

"Let's just hope we don't get *caught*," Aiden amended. "What's in that big box?"

Miguel lit another match and went over to investigate. "Hey, Eagledink. What does T-N-T spell?"

"Put out that match!" rasped Aiden in a panic.

Miguel nearly choked on his laughter. "You are such a sucker! It's just some old tarps. Our beds, dummy."

Beside him, Aiden heard Meg snicker.

There was an abrupt lurch and a screech from the steel wheels. The train began to creep forwards.

Miguel shared out the tarpaulins. They were

rough and stiff and smelled strongly of cabbages. To the fugitives, they were the softest of perfumed feather beds.

All three were asleep before the train had gathered full speed.

"Aiden — time to get your shoes on."

Six-year-old Aiden Falconer sat cross-legged on the shag carpeting of his small bedroom in the summerhouse. Spread out on the floor in front of him were a dozen colour photographs, the boy's pride and joy. He had taken them himself, using his own camera, and his very first roll of film.

"Come on, Aiden. We have to be at the Colchester Grill at six."

"I'm busy," he called down the stairs. He hated restaurants where you had to sit in your chair the whole time, waiting for ever for people to bring food you weren't going to like anyway. They never had hamburgers. And pretty soon Meg would be crying.

"Uncle Frank and Aunt Jane will wonder what happened to us."

"I'm not going." He selected a single picture out of his array — Uncle Frank and Aunt Jane. They were nice enough, he supposed, but so boring. Whenever they

were around, all Mom and Dad wanted to do was talk.
And eat dinner for three hours.

He prepared to rip the snapshot into a billion pieces.
But he could hear his mother's footsteps starting up the
stairs. Quickly, he collected his pictures, stuffed them
into the cigar box that held his summer treasures, and
stashed that in his secret hiding place. He got the loose
piece of panel back in its slot just as his mother burst
into the room.

"What is the matter with you, Aiden? We are going
out to dinner, and that's that."

She reached down and hoisted him high in the air. As
he swung around past the window, he saw the gleaming
waters of Lake Champlain on a summer afternoon. The
dock was festooned with hundreds of coloured flags. At
the near end, the ferry was boarding for its trip to the
New York side of the lake.

"Come on, sweetie," his mother coaxed. "You'll have
fun."

As she held him, he had a strange feeling that he
should be hugging her harder, never letting go. . .

Aiden awoke sucking air, because someone had
taken his mother away, and she was never coming
back.

"Hey – Eagledink!" Miguel was shaking him.

Aiden sat up in the darkness of the boxcar. The dream was still very real in his mind. *Colchester. The house was in Colchester, Vermont.*

Miguel brayed a derisive laugh. "You were crying for Mommy. You've got some serious hang-ups about your folks. What gives?"

Aiden looked around, orientating himself. A thin line of light showed at the edge of the sliding door. Daylight. He checked his watch: 4.05.

We've been asleep for eleven hours!

"Meg?"

"Still snoozing," said Miguel.

"No, I'm not," came her drowsy voice. "Where are we?"

"Stopped," Aiden said. It was only then that he realized it himself. The train was standing still. He turned to Miguel. "How long have we been stopped?"

"Don't know. I've been sleeping like you."

They could hear voices outside – Aiden listened – strident voices, barking orders. The rumble and slam of boxcar doors kept repeating itself, and – was that a siren?

"Something's up," Meg said nervously.

Miguel slid the door open a few inches and flattened himself so he could peer up the length of the train. "Cops," he said.

Aiden was horrified. "Searching the train?"

"No, dancing the hula. Get a grip!"

"*You* get a grip!" Aiden hissed angrily. "This is *your* fault! They probably saw the busted candy machine in Gibbon and knew we were on this freight!"

"Can we run for it?" Meg interrupted.

Miguel shook his head. "They're too close. We're trapped."

10

Trapped in a boxcar.

Something frantic rattled around in Aiden's head. He should know about this! This was familiar.

That's crazy! You've never been on a train that wasn't a commuter. What do you know about escaping from a freight car?

Then he remembered. Mac Mulvey, Dad's recurring detective hero, had once broken out of a locked freezer car via—

He looked up and there it was. The shaft of light from the open slider shone on an emergency hatch in the ceiling. He rushed over to the wooden crate and began positioning it in the centre of the car.

"What are you going to do, Eagledink?" scoffed Miguel. "Mail yourself out of here?"

Aiden pointed straight up. Instantly, he had two helpers. When the crate was in place, he scrambled up the wooden side and balanced on the narrow rim. The trapdoor was held in place by a small latch. He popped the hatch, reached up, and took hold of the roof of the car.

Here goes, he thought. If the police were watching the top of the train, this would be his last act as a free person. *One . . . two . . .* — a silent prayer — *three!*

He heaved himself up through the opening and flopped flat on to the metal surface. He could see tall buildings in the distance — a skyline. They were outside a big city. But their immediate surroundings were lower and leafier. This was a suburban station. To his left, about a dozen cops patrolled the platform, searching the train. And they were only *two cars away*!

"Hurry!" he hissed, reaching down to help Meg and then Miguel to the roof of the boxcar.

He looked around desperately. To his right was an empty track. There weren't any officers on that side. But it was a twelve-foot drop to the ground.

A broken ankle — not a good idea for a fugitive.

"Follow me," he whispered.

Keeping low, he slithered forward on the metal roof, scrambling over the four-foot gap to the next car. Over his shoulder, he could see Miguel and Meg following him. The three snaked silently ahead, barely daring to breathe. Soon Aiden found himself on a different kind of surface – a thick lattice cage.

The powerful farm odour reached him almost immediately. A livestock carrier. Animals' lowing wafted up from below.

He peered down through the bars. Didn't it figure?

Cows.

He slunk to the edge of the car and eased over the side. Using the steel struts as ladder rungs, he began to climb down. The cows mooed at him; one even pressed its snout right up to the opening and licked him. But he was able to clamber low enough to jump to the ground.

Miguel landed beside him a few seconds later. Meg came last. As her sneakers made contact with the gravel, she lost her footing and lurched towards the open track. Miguel grabbed her arm and propped her back into balance.

He gestured meaningfully at the spot where she had almost fallen. This was a commuter line. It had an electrified third rail. Had Meg touched it, she would have been seriously injured or even killed.

Her mouth formed the word "thanks", but she allowed no sound to come out.

Hidden behind the bulk of the train, they scampered the length of the station. A small metal ladder provided access to the outbound platform. They scrambled up, trying to look like local kids and not fleeing felons.

They were in luck. The vacant side was nearly deserted. At this time of day, people returning from a day's work in the city just wanted to get home. No one was hanging around.

They strode purposefully towards the stairway to the parking lot. It was a hundred yards away – a single football field. For the first time, Aiden allowed the notion to enter his mind that they might survive this latest close call.

They were halfway there – the fifty-yard line – when the toilet door opened and out stepped a pudgy, middle-aged policeman. It was too late to turn, too late to hide. The only plan of action was to keep walking. As they drew close, Aiden noticed the fax in the officer's hand. The page was dotted with photographs – murky mugshots of the Sunnydale runaways.

Strangely – amazingly – the cop let them pass. They forged on, eyes fixed straight ahead. Was it possible that he simply hadn't noticed them?

Leather soles scraping against concrete – the

sound of someone turning around. Then: "Hey! *Hey!!*"

They ran, flying across the platform and down the stairs. The cop gave chase. "Police! Hey! Stop!"

In addition to being tougher than the Falconers, Miguel turned out to be faster as well. He blasted through the parking lot, opening a gap between himself and Aiden and Meg.

He'll get away and we won't! The thought brought Aiden hidden reserves of power, and he turned on the jets and kept pace. Meg was hot on his heels.

Luckily, the policeman wasn't much of an athlete. They could hear him puffing into his walkie-talkie: "Lewin to Caldwell . . . Chris, I've got 'em . . . fast little rats."

The parking lot was bordered by a small strip of stores and restaurants. Beyond that, subdivisions began.

Miguel never hesitated. He barreled headlong down tree-lined roads, wheeling left and right, navigating as if he'd lived here all his life.

The Falconers followed like the tail of a comet. They had no loyalty for Miguel Reyes; they didn't like him, and trusted him zero. But he ran with the kind of cool self-assurance that inspired confidence. Besides, if anybody was an expert at fleeing the police, it had to be this juvenile delinquent. For good or ill, their fates had become intertwined.

Aiden looked over his shoulder. He could no longer see Officer Lewin. It brought some relief, but reinforcements couldn't be far behind.

Miguel sensed that, for the moment, the coast was clear. He selected one of the scores of identical homes and dashed for it, hopping the fence with an effortless vault.

Aiden was practically babbling as he scrambled over the obstacle. "What are you doing? There's nowhere to hide here!"

Miguel indicated the house, a well-tended brick colonial surrounded by sculpted bushes. "What do you call that?"

Meg jumped down beside them. "A houseful of people," she panted. "With a telephone for calling the police."

"For a couple of Eagles, you guys are blind as bats. There's a pile of newspapers on the front doorstep. They're on *vacation*, brainiacs. Nobody home. No alarm, either."

"How do you know?" puffed Aiden.

"No stickers in the windows. Alarm people love stickers." He pulled a grapefruit-sized stone out of the garden and headed for the patio doors.

The Falconers exchanged uneasy glances. Taking clothes from a drying rack or bikes that you planned to return was one thing. *This* was breaking and entering.

But pretty soon the whole neighbourhood will be crawling with cops!

Amazing, Aiden marvelled. The only way to survive as a fugitive was by breaking even more laws.

If the police really want to reduce crime, they should leave us alone.

Miguel hefted the rock and deftly punched out a single pane of glass from the French doors. He reached inside and flipped the latch.

They were in.

11

They cleaned up the glass and took in the telltale newspapers. The next order of business, according to Miguel, was their appearance.

"What's wrong with how we look?" asked Aiden.

"Well, you're both pretty ugly," Miguel wisecracked, "but that's not the problem. We match our mugshots, yo. Cops'll make us in a heartbeat."

He rustled through a few kitchen cabinets and drawers and came up with a pair of scissors. "Who's first?"

"No way," Meg said firmly. "I'm not letting this lunatic touch my hair."

Miguel shrugged. "No skin off my back, little sis. More time for me to split while the cops are cuffing you."

"There's too much at stake to risk getting caught," Aiden told her.

Meg hesitated. "You ever cut hair before?" she asked Miguel.

"I'm Vin Diesel's personal barber."

"Aiden—"

Aiden sighed. "Just do it."

Meg sat on a kitchen chair, biting back rage, as clumps of her long dark hair scattered on the floor. When she finally regarded herself in the mirror, she almost cried. She looked like a *geek*, with a bob cut that exposed her ears.

"You should stick to murder," she mumbled bitterly, "because as a stylist, you stink."

"*Hey!*" Miguel was upon her in an instant, grabbing a fistful of T-shirt and pushing her hard against the refrigerator. She felt the scissor blade pressing on the skin of her neck. "Don't you *ever* call me a murderer! You hear me?"

With cold steel against her throat, Meg was too petrified to reply.

"Let her go, man!" cried Aiden, struggling to remain calm. "She didn't mean it!"

Miguel's eyes burned feverishly. "It was *manslaughter*!"

"We know that," Aiden soothed. "We're all friends here. We've got to stick together if we're going to get out of this, right?"

"They don't send murderers to milk cows!"

Miguel made no move to release her. "You do hard time for that!"

"We *know*!"

The scissors hit the tile floor with a clatter. Meg fled to her brother's arms. The message flashed between them: *who's the real enemy — the police or Miguel?*

"It was manslaughter," the olive-skinned boy repeated to no one in particular. Then, his voice barely audible, he added, "Jerk had it coming, anyway."

Soon Aiden's curly top had been reduced to a tight crew cut. Meg was amazed at how his entire appearance was transformed. Her brother had always had a serious yet somehow goofy look to him. Now his cheekbones seemed higher, his jaw stronger, his eyes more deep set. His appearance was older, more mature. Could one haircut have done all this, she wondered? Or had life on the run already aged her brother?

They found a box of colour formula in the upstairs bathroom. While Aiden dyed his fair hair jet-black, Meg massaged hydrogen peroxide into the bob. Her scalp stung like crazy, but twenty painful minutes later she was a platinum blonde.

Miguel gave himself a quick haircut using a portable sideburn trimmer. He loved the new him so much that he paid the trimmer the ultimate compliment – he pocketed it.

Meg started to protest . . . and then the doorbell rang.

A lightning strike could not have produced such electricity inside the house. Meg ran to the window, hoping against hope that she wouldn't see what she knew she would – a police cruiser, parked at the kerb.

Miguel saw it, too. "Heat."

Aiden was well on his way to panic. "Why'd you have to take in those newspapers?" he confronted Miguel. "Now they know somebody's here!"

"They'd check an empty house twice as close, Eagledink," Miguel retorted. "Maybe notice that missing glass out back."

The doorbell rang twice more. Meg could hear urgency in its tone. Sucking in a breath, she headed downstairs.

Aiden realized his sister's intentions too late. "Don't do it!"

But Meg just knew, although she wasn't sure how: *don't give the cops a chance to snoop around.*

And there was only one way to do that.

She threw open the door and peered up at a tall, thin officer. Her heart nearly stopped when she saw he was holding a faxed page with their mugshots.

Get out of here! Slam the door and run!

Yet there was no recognition in the young cop's eyes.

He smiled at her. "Pardon the intrusion, son. Is your mom home?"

Meg struggled to conceal her amazement. He thought she was a *boy*!

She conjured her best shy expression. "My parents are at work," she mumbled, peering alternately at the officer and the floor. *Don't let him get a good look at you. . .*

"You're kind of young to be here all alone," the cop said kindly. "Who's watching you?"

"Carolyn. My sister. She's fourteen."

"Maybe I should talk with her."

"Sure," Meg agreed. "But you'll have to wait till she gets out of the shower. She takes, like, twenty showers a day." She wrinkled her nose. "Girls do that."

The cop grinned. "So I've heard. Have you seen anybody suspicious in the neighbourhood the last couple of hours? Big kids, teenagers – two boys and a girl?"

She shook her head. "Burglars?"

"Nothing to get worked up over," he reassured her. "Just keep the house locked until your folks get home. And if you see anybody suspicious, you know the number to call, right?"

"Nine-one-one?" she ventured, almost too timidly.

"Good boy. Sorry to bother you." He started down the walk, tossing one last sentence over his shoulder. "Have your folks call the station if they have any questions."

When the door clicked shut, Meg nearly collapsed with relief.

Aiden and Miguel stepped out from behind the wall, regarding her in open mouthed wonder.

Aiden was white with fear. "Are you nuts? What if he wanted to chat with big sister Carolyn?"

Meg shrugged, not managing to look as cool as she'd hoped. "He didn't."

Miguel was staring at her with a new light in his eyes, something neither Falconer had seen before. Respect?

"Little sis," he said, "you've got it going on!"

Miguel couldn't find any money to steal, but he did unearth some travel confirmations. The MacKinnons of 144 Purple Sage Path, Hillside Park, Illinois, were at Disney World. They had flown United, rented from Hertz, and were staying at the Grand Floridian while the Sunnydale escapees "borrowed" their home.

"He's not just a thief and a killer," Meg whispered to Aiden. "He's also a pretty decent spy."

With the family on vacation, the house was empty of food except for three frozen pizzas – all gone by the time *Judge Judy* came on television.

"The legacy of Sunnydale," Aiden observed. "We can watch anything, no matter how boring."

"Bring on Dr Phil," agreed Meg.

Miguel had a complaint. "Compared to my brother's set-up, this dinky screen is a postage stamp."

The looting of the upstairs bedrooms was next. The MacKinnons had four children, and there were clothes for everyone. To Miguel's humiliation, he was a perfect fit for Mrs MacKinnon's shoes.

He set to work in the garage blackening a pair of ladies' Reeboks with a tube of General Motors touch-up paint. Aiden and Meg channel surfed in the den, searching for details on the hunt for the Sunnydale escapees.

The Chicago news did a short account of the chase at the train station, but it was sandwiched between local crime pieces. CNN had nothing, although the scrolling updates at the bottom of the screen did mention that all but six of the missing juvenile offenders had been apprehended.

"I wonder who the other three are," mused Aiden.

"That's so like you, bro," Meg told him. "You worry about the wrong stuff. Who cares who else made it? *We* made it; that's all that matters. The big question is how do we get to Vermont from here? And —" she dropped her voice to a whisper — "how do we get away from that maniac? The sooner we kiss off Miguel, the sooner we can both breathe easier."

Aiden hesitated. He wasn't convinced that splitting from Miguel was the wisest course for them. As fugitives, the Falconers were completely clueless, flying by the seat of their pants. Miguel, on the other hand, had experience living outside the law. Yes, he was dangerous. But he might be a valuable guide.

For a while, anyway.

Miguel strolled into the room, modelling the painted Reeboks. "Check it out. I must be bad or something."

"Bad isn't the half of it," Meg muttered.

"Cheer up, little sis. You should be smiling. Why don't you ask me how we're going to get out of here?"

Aiden came alive. "You have a plan?"

In answer, Miguel jingled a set of car keys.

"But –" Meg was incredulous – "we don't know how to drive!"

"Speak for yourself. I was boosting rides when you were still playing with Barbies."

"Absolutely not," Aiden said firmly. "Come on, Miguel, these poor people! We break into their house, eat their food, steal their clothes. We're not going to rip off their car. No way!"

Dear Mr and Mrs MacKinnon,
There's probably not much we can say to make you forgive us for what we did to you. We're very sorry, but we had no choice. Someday, if things

work out, we hope we can pay you back. Trust
me, no one wants that more than we do. . .

The car horn echoed through the house like an air
raid siren.

"Our chauffeur awaits," Meg commented dryly.

Aiden was still staring at the paper. *It's the only
way,* he thought, convincing himself for at least the
fifth time. *The cops will be expecting us to hop a train
or bus. This is our ticket out, our ticket east. . .*

More honking. Hurriedly, he scribbled the rest of
the note:

Please believe me – this is not how we usually
are. We're not bad people but we're DESPERATE!!!

He put down the pen and said, "Let's go."

Miguel grinned down from the wheel of a black
Chevy Tahoe. "You navigate," he told Aiden, indi-
cating a tattered map spread across the passenger
seat. Meg climbed into the back.

They had delayed their departure until cover of
darkness. Opening the garage door flooded Purple
Sage Path with blazing light.

They can probably see us from the space shuttle!
Aiden thought nervously.

94

Now that the moment had arrived, abandoning their refuge seemed reckless and insane. Inside the MacKinnons' house, they were safe. Outside, anything could happen.

"Watch it," Meg exclaimed as the heavy SUV bounced over the kerbstones. "You're on the lawn!"

Miguel snorted in glee. "This is grand theft auto! Gonna yell at me for tyre marks on the grass?" He shifted out of reverse and roared off.

Navigation was bedlam, with Meg calling out street names and Aiden poring over the map, trying to place them in the spaghetti of roads and highways. The chaos just made Miguel laugh harder and drive faster. He was having the time of his life.

Nothing like an A-felony to bring out your inner child.

All at once, Meg cried, "Elmhurst Road – turn left!"

Miguel yanked on the wheel, and there it was – the entrance to the interstate, half a mile ahead. Flashing lights played off the tops of a parking lot of stopped cars clogging the roadway. There, before the ramp, were stationed four uniformed policemen, shining flashlights into windshields.

Aiden's formless fears suddenly crystallized with a crunch. "Roadblock!" he rasped.

Meg was incredulous "For *us*? But—" Her reasoning crumbled to dust. Of course the police would be expecting them to make a break for it. And where would the cops look? Freeway entrances near the spot where the fugitives were last seen.

Miguel threw the Tahoe into reverse, but it was too late. There were already several cars behind them.

Aiden looked around frantically. On their left, a two-foot-high concrete barrier separated them from oncoming traffic. On the right was a huge construction site – a deep ditch that took up an entire city block. "They've got us," he groaned.

"They've got squat," said Miguel, shutting off the headlights. With a grinding of gears, he shifted into four-wheel drive, swung out of the line of cars, and gunned the engine.

The Tahoe roared off the edge of the excavation. They were airborne, unconnected to anything on the ground. Through his horror and disbelief, Aiden felt gravity take over from the force of the car's forward momentum. They were falling.

The SUV lurched as its tyres made contact with the dirt truck ramp. They rattled across the mud and rocks of the ditch, swerving at the last second to avoid cement mixers and portable generators.

Aiden peered out the back window. "I don't think anybody's following us. Hey, how'd you know that truck ramp was going to be there?"

Miguel's gaze never wavered from the obstacle course of construction equipment. "I didn't."

At the far side of the site, another ramp led back to street level. No sirens or flashing lights awaited them there.

They had dodged the bullet.

They crossed the city by dimly lit surface roads. They would have to get on the freeway eventually, but the metro area was an awfully large haystack, and three kids in a Tahoe represented a single needle. The Chicago grid hid them all the way to the Indiana border.

Later, as they stopped for a toilet break, Meg whispered to her brother: "This guy was ready to drive off a twenty-foot cliff. We've got to ditch him before he gets us killed."

Aiden was toying with the idea that the opposite might be true. If they were to have a prayer of helping their parents, they would have to watch Miguel, to learn from him, almost *be* him in a sense.

To survive as a fugitive, you have to be a little bit crazy.

For the next two hundred miles, Aiden and Meg peered out the rear window of the Tahoe, expecting to see a line of police cruisers closing in on them, sirens wailing. But after a while, even fear becomes a routine emotion. Meg fell asleep just west of Toledo, Ohio. And somewhere along the south shore of Lake Erie, Aiden, too, surrendered to his overpowering fatigue.

Fevered dreams gave him little peace. Even as every broken line on the asphalt drew them closer to the east and their past with Frank Lindenauer, Aiden's time-faded memory tried and failed to paint a picture of the family friend who was the Falconers' CIA contact. The photograph – he could see the snapshot, but the face remained blank.

And the questions. Always the questions.

Why hadn't Lindenauer come forward during the trial? Was he sick? Dead? Suffering from amnesia? Or living in some isolated cabin where he simply hadn't heard about the Falconers' plight?

Oh, come on. He knew. Everybody knew. CNN called it the trial of the new millennium!

Why had he hung his friends out to dry that way? The one person who could have proved they were innocent. . .

If they were innocent—

How can you think that? Of course they're innocent! Does Meg ever have the slightest doubt about Mom and Dad? What kind of son are you?

"Eagledink." Miguel was shaking his shoulder.

"I'm awake." The digital readout said 3.34 a.m. Chicago time – 4.34 in the east. They were pulling into a highway service area. In the darkness, he could make out a few other cars and a lot of big rigs – truckers taking advantage of the empty roads. "Why are we stopping?"

"Gas," Miguel told him. "We should've boosted something with a little more fuel efficiency."

"We're broke," Aiden mused.

"We were stupid," Miguel commented. "We should've swiped some jewellery out of that house, pawned it in Chicago."

Aiden fought down his natural revulsion to crime. *This is your new reality. Get used to it.*

99

He said, "If we can steal earrings, we can steal gas. Just fill up and fly, right?"

Miguel shook his head. "Place like this, they've got cameras on the pumps. They'd radio our plate numbers to every cop between here and the George Washington Bridge. What we need is a credit card."

"Where do we get one of those?"

Miguel fluttered his fingers. "I have hidden talents."

Aiden was appalled. "Rip off somebody's wallet and buy gas while he's still looking for it?"

"You got a better idea, Eagledink?"

Aiden thought he had. Or at least his father had — in the continuing adventures of Mac Mulvey.

Meg jolted awake in the back of the Tahoe, groggy and disorientated. "Where are we?"

"Getting gas," Miguel replied.

She sat up. "I'm going to the toilets."

"It's not that kind of pit stop."

"Huh?" They were nowhere near the gas pumps. The Tahoe was parked in the middle of a covey of transport trucks, hidden from the main station. She squinted out the window. Aiden was stringing a garden hose between the SUV and a large box van. "What's he doing?"

Miguel rolled his eyes. "He gave me some lecture about science. I told him to go jack the Magic School Bus—"

Now Aiden had one end of the hose in his mouth. Suddenly, he yanked it free. Pale liquid spewed from the nozzle. He jammed it in the Tahoe's fuel door.

"He's siphoning from the truck!" Meg exclaimed in amazement. "It's higher than us, so once he starts the gas moving, gravity will empty it into our tank!"

Miguel was impressed. "Maybe I should've paid attention in school."

Aiden appeared nervous but triumphant as fuel from the much larger box van drained into the SUV.

And then a fist the size of a small ham closed on his shoulder.

A force several times his own strength yanked him away from the Tahoe. The siphoning hose came loose, spewing a fountain of gas. Aiden wheeled to find himself grappling with the driver of the truck, a cement head and shovel jaw atop a broad ridge of plaid shoulders.

Aiden managed to spin himself free, only to be locked in the crushing bear hug of a second lumberjack type.

"Aiden!" Meg sprang for the door handle. But

Miguel started the engine and stomped on the accelerator. The Tahoe squealed ahead, narrowly threading the needle between a tanker truck and a lumber trailer.

The burst of speed plastered Meg against the door. "What are you doing?" she shrieked. "Go back!"

"He's done! Forget him!"

"*No!*"

Miguel aimed the Tahoe at the exit ramp that led to the interstate. "What do you think those guys'll do when they're through working him over? They'll turn him in! You want to go back into the system — a place with bars instead of chickens this time?"

"I'm not leaving!"

"I'm not asking!"

They were on the ramp now. In another few seconds they would be hurtling east on the freeway, abandoning Aiden to a beating and, worse, capture. Unable to think of anything else to do, Meg reached around the seat and clamped both hands over Miguel's eyes.

There was a cry of outrage as he batted them away. "You trying to get us killed?"

She lunged again, locking both arms around his

head. He struggled but could not budge her. "Are you *crazy*?"

She held on, wondering if she really *was* crazy. In another thirty feet they'd be on the interstate, surrounded by speeding cars. . .

At the last moment, Miguel stomped on the brakes. The Tahoe spun out of control and lurched to a stop at the end of the ramp. Meg tumbled head over heels, landing on the floor mat in front of the passenger seat.

He glowered at her. "I've got no problem pitching you out that door *this minute*! You think I need some little girl slowing me down?"

Shaken and terrified, Meg glared right back into the teeth of his rage. "I'll crash the two of us, don't think I won't! *I'm not leaving my brother!*"

14

The punch in the gut knocked the wind out of Aiden, leaving him wheezing. The bigger of the two truckers held him in a full nelson, cursing and calling him every kind of punk in the book. The other man was more concerned with removing the siphoning hose from the box van's fuel tank.

Aiden knew he would never have a better chance. He brought his head forward and then snapped it back into his captor's shovel jaw. There were two grunts of pain — one of them from Aiden himself. The hold relaxed, and he exploded out of the tree-trunk arms.

The lumberjack brothers took off after him. But Aiden was flying, his high-stepping feet splashing in the puddled petroleum.

One thing I've gotten good at — running for my life.

Soon he was halfway across the parking lot. The question remained: where was he running *to*? What could he do — hide in the woods outside some interstate truck stop? Miguel and Meg were gone, and he had no way to find them.

Then he saw it. Down the service area's exit ramp, the Tahoe was backing up at fifty miles an hour. He could see his sister's white face in the window and Miguel peering over his shoulder as he reversed at top speed.

Aiden waved his arms. "Over here!"

They came perilously close to flattening him. Meg threw open the rear door and he leaped inside.

Miguel put the SUV in drive and they squealed off towards the highway. "I thought *I* was bugging, but you Eagles are loony tunes."

Meg lashed out at Miguel, pummelling his arm and shoulder.

He deflected the blows into the dashboard. The windshield wipers jumped to life and the radio came on. "I went back, didn't I?"

Meg was out of control, spluttering tears of rage. "He was going to *leave* you!"

"I was caught—" Aiden reasoned.

"*Traitor!*" she roared at Miguel.

And then a newscaster's voice spoke a very familiar name, "Sunnydale."

"*Quiet!*" ordered Aiden.

Silence fell in the SUV.

". . .*all but three of the missing residents are once again in custody,*" the woman was saying. "*Still at large are fifteen-year-old Miguel Reyes, and a brother and sister registered under the name Eagleson. The Department of Juvenile Corrections has just confirmed that the Eaglesons are, in fact, Aiden and Margaret Falconer, ages fifteen and eleven, children of convicted traitors John and Louise Falconer.*"

Miguel pulled the Tahoe on to the shoulder in a screech of burning rubber. He turned on his passengers, eyes wide. "That's *you*?" he asked in horror. "Your parents are *terrorists*?"

"No—" Aiden began.

"But they helped terrorists. And you're calling *me* a traitor?"

"They're innocent!" Meg stormed.

"Innocent?" Miguel spat. "What does that mean? Remember Sunnydale? We were *all* innocent. Every place I've been — you can't find anybody guilty. If you go by the people doing time, crime is nothing but an ugly rumour started by a bunch of cops."

Meg was becoming belligerent. "Our parents were framed, and we're going to prove it!"

Understanding struck Miguel. "So *that's* the plan. You're going to ride in on white horses and rescue Mommy and Daddy."

"No," Aiden said patiently. "We're going to find evidence to clear their names."

"You're dreaming."

"Maybe," Aiden agreed. "But what else can we do? You know of another way to get justice?"

"Justice!" Miguel practically snarled the word. "You rich kids are all the same. Why are you entitled to justice? Where's my justice?"

"It's not the same thing," Aiden argued. "Maybe you had a good reason for what you did, but you still did it."

Miguel pulled out into traffic. When he spoke, his eyes were riveted to the horizon. He wouldn't so much as glance at Aiden or Meg.

"Yeah, I'm a real cold-blooded killer. Know what I'm guilty of? Shoving. Felony shoving. Aggravated shoving. First-degree shoving. If you lived with my stepfather, you'd be sick of being his punching bag, too. How was I supposed to know the jerk was going to fall down the stairs? Cops said he broke his neck – killed instantly."

"*That's* what happened?" Meg exclaimed in amazement. "You just defended yourself? You're innocent!"

"Don't you get it?" Miguel asked bitterly. "There's no innocent and guilty, just lucky and unlucky. Think my old lady's going to blow her savings on a lawyer for the kid who put her husband in the cemetery? Unlucky – same as your folks."

Aiden was thunderstruck. "Miguel – I don't know what to say. Being in jail for something you didn't even do – we both know what that's like."

Miguel twisted the radio dial, searching for music. "Listen, Eagle – Falcon – whoever you are. This car's rolling to my brother's place. Come, don't come – it makes no difference to me. But if New Jersey isn't in your travel plans, now's the time to do something about it."

Aiden and Meg said nothing. But as the Tahoe continued its long journey east, neither made any move to get out.

At the Department of Juvenile Corrections in Washington, DC, Agent Emmanuel Harris strode past the secretary without stopping.

"Sir!" she shrilled. "Deputy Director Adler can't be disturbed—"

Harris threw open the door, ducking so his head would clear the frame. "You *knew*," he accused, pointing a missile-like index finger at the thirty-something bureaucrat behind the desk. "You *knew* the Falconers were at Sunnydale. And you knew they were missing five minutes after that place went up in smoke."

"Sure, I did." In an attempt to look older, Adler sported a patchy moustache that almost – but not quite – filled in the space above his upper lip. "I also knew that information was classified for the kids' own good."

The famous sarcasm. "Yeah, we did them a real favour, throwing them in jail—"

"It's not a jail," the deputy director interrupted.

"No," Harris agreed. "From what I hear, it's a pile of charcoal."

"Aiden and Margaret Falconer were never in the system. They were at Sunnydale for their own protection."

"Surrounded by lowlifes," Harris added. "Like this Reyes kid with manslaughter on his rap sheet."

"They're not the little angels you think they are. They escaped from federal custody—"

"I thought they were never in the system."

"—and we're charging the boy with arson. We have an eyewitness who says he deliberately started the fire with a kerosene lamp."

"A kerosene lamp?" the agent exploded. "What is this, the dark ages?"

"Hard work and a simple life is a proven approach in dealing with young offenders," the deputy director said stoutly. "Don't tell me my job."

"You're not *doing* your job," Harris insisted. "You need to find these kids before they get hurt."

"We'll track them down," Adler said confidently. "We traced them from a couple of stolen bikes to the train station in Gibbon, Nebraska. The next day, they were spotted outside Chicago. The local cops set up roadblocks, but somehow the kids dropped off the radar. They had hooked up with Reyes by then."

Harris took a deep breath. "Suppose I can bring them in before they get into any more trouble. Could you look the other way on the fire? It was probably an accident anyway. What kid today knows how to use a kerosene lamp? You might as well hand him a flamethrower."

The deputy director regarded his lofty visitor with genuine interest. "You knocked off the biggest treason case in half a century. You're a hero in the FBI with a big future. Why can't you let go of these two kids?"

"Because I created them, that's why!" Harris snapped. "I made them what they are today – motherless, fatherless, homeless fugitives. Can't you get it through your head? Everything that happens to Aiden and Margaret Falconer – it's on me!"

Aiden had never been to New York City, but he recognized the skyline instantly from pictures and TV. As the tops of the gleaming towers sprouted from New Jersey's horizon, he allowed himself the tiniest breath of relief.

The East. We made it.

The nightmare of their near miss in Chicago was

111

over. From here, the country's busiest hub, trains and buses connected passengers to every conceivable destination. Including Vermont.

Miguel had become bubbly the minute they'd crossed over from Pennsylvania. "Wait till you see the sweet set-up Freddy's got – flat-screen TV, surround sound, quicksand couch – you *sink* into those pillows!"

Now the Falconers were his best buddies. The bullying and intimidation evaporated the closer they got to his brother's house. For Aiden, the picture of Miguel holding a pair of scissors to Meg's throat wasn't likely to fade any time soon. But he had to admit that life in the Tahoe was certainly more pleasant when Miguel was in a good mood.

Union City, New Jersey, reminded Aiden of *The King of Queens* – endless tracts of long, narrow houses stacked close together like dominoes. Miguel pulled into the driveway of one of a row of identical cracker boxes.

"A millionth of a tank of gas to spare!" he declared triumphantly. He was positively beaming.

This was it – the end of the line for Miguel. Aiden was surprised at the lump in his throat. As nasty and unpredictable as Miguel was, it was comforting to have a partner who knew the ropes. Without him, the Falconers would be totally on their own.

So they allowed themselves to be coaxed up the front walk. "You guys kick back, maybe watch a movie, while I talk to Freddy. He's a smart guy. He can help you get where you're going."

A young dark woman who was very pregnant answered the door. "Angie!" cried Miguel, enfolding her in a big bear hug. "Look at you, girl! Why didn't Freddy tell me?"

Aiden couldn't help noticing that Angie did not seem happy at the sight of the newcomers. "Come in, come in," she said furtively, rushing to shut the door behind them. "*Freddy, we got company!*"

Miguel didn't pick up on her discomfort. "So, when's the baby due?"

"Uh – three weeks. *Freddy!*"

The house was small and shabby, with cracked plaster walls dividing the space into tiny rooms. At the end of the hall, Aiden could see an enormous TV screen – the subject of Miguel's endless bragging at Sunnydale.

"You *idiot*!"

Coming down the stairs was a man in his early

113

twenties – an older version of Miguel on a sturdier, more muscular frame. Despite the similarities in appearance, their expressions could not have been more different. Freddy Reyes was an unhealthy shade of purple.

"Are you crazy, coming here? Bringing *them* –" pointing at the Falconers. "Did anybody tell you who their parents are?"

"They're my friends," Miguel said defensively. "You know how it is when you're with people on the inside."

"Didn't you think the cops would come to me when you went on the lam?" Freddy demanded. "They've been here three times already, and that's just when they've knocked on the door! Angie and me – we see them cruising by, keeping an eye on the place."

Aiden felt his heart lurch. Any passing police officer would find a stolen SUV parked in plain sight on the driveway.

"I'll move the car," Miguel promised. "Park it on another street. I'll be careful."

"You'll be more than careful!" Freddy thundered. "You'll be *gone*!"

"What are you talking about, Fred?"

"You can't stay here, man! I'm still on parole. If they catch me with you, I'm back in the can. I can't risk that – not with a kid coming!"

The blow was so hard, so unexpected, that even Aiden felt the sting. For Miguel, coming to New Jersey to live with his brother had always been the pot of gold at the end of the rainbow. He had contemplated it, fantasized about it, obsessed over it – in custody, and on every mile of their long flight from Nebraska. And now the dream was in ashes, just like the juvenile detention facility that had once held him.

Miguel was shattered. "That's crazy, Freddy!" He searched his brother's face for some sign of softening. There was none. "Well, what about Ma? Could I stay with her?"

"Ma's on antidepressants – like she has been ever since you whacked her husband. I swear, Miguel – you go over there, and I'll beat your lousy head in. Leave us all alone – you're not part of this family any more!"

"But –" It was barely a whisper. "What am I going to do? I've got nowhere to go. No money—"

Freddy pulled a wad of cash out of his pocket, peeled off a couple of bills for himself, and pressed the rest into his brother's palm. "I wish it could be different, kid, but you gotta get lost. If anybody asks, you never saw me."

Miguel stared blankly down at the bills in his hand. It would have been impossible to tell he was crying, if not for the trembling of his shoulders. One time at Sunnydale, Gary Donovan had smacked him with a planting spade hard enough to open a four-inch gash on his head — sixty stitches. Miguel never uttered a peep. Aiden remembered thinking that no amount of pain would ever get tears out of this guy.

I was wrong.

Miguel might have stood rooted to the spot forever if Meg hadn't taken his arm and led him out of the house. He followed meekly, without protest.

Aiden brought up the rear, but at the door, he turned angry eyes on the elder Reyes. It was stupid, he knew. He always criticized Meg for speaking up out of pure brash emotion, when no good could possibly come of it. But this had to be said.

"Ever heard of self-defence?" he challenged. "Big family man — why didn't you get a decent lawyer for your own brother? Better yet, why didn't you keep your stepfather off him before it came to that?"

Freddy's eyes bulged. "I should turn you in right now!"

But Aiden was already on the cement path back to the car.

Miguel slumped in the Tahoe's passenger seat, his head lolling against its rest. He reminded Aiden of an old *Far Side* cartoon of a boneless chicken ranch, with formless poultry flopping limply around a farmyard.

But there's nothing funny about Miguel's life right now.

Meg was trying to urge him behind the wheel. "We've got to get out of here. You heard Freddy. The cops could come around any minute."

"I got nowhere to go," mumbled Miguel. "Back into the system – that's as good a place as anywhere else."

Aiden would not have believed he'd ever be capable of such sympathy towards the bully who had once made a career of tormenting him. Yet he recognized Miguel's despair almost instantly. It was the combination of misery and hopelessness Aiden and Meg had felt during the trial, in the foster homes, and at Sunnydale. He knew from bitter experience that nothing he could do would cheer Miguel up.

The best he could hope for was to show the boy he wasn't completely alone.

"There's a lake house in Colchester, Vermont," he said slowly. "Our old summer cottage. We think there might be a clue there – a picture of a guy who can prove our parents are innocent."

It felt good to say it out loud – almost as if discussing it made it real.

Not just the distant memory of a six-year-old.

"What's your point, Falcon?" Miguel groaned. "It's been a rough day."

Meg supplied the answer. "Are you up for a road trip?"

Aiden Falconer had never driven a car in his life. Now he had no choice. Miguel was utterly defeated and deflated. Once the terror of kids who were terrors themselves, he now couldn't muster the will to haul himself out of the Tahoe's passenger seat. So Aiden took over the wheel.

He had no licence, of course – he was only fifteen. But that was minor compared with the stack of crimes he and Meg had committed so far. Even *that* seemed small in the face of their larger mission. Vermont was just a few hundred miles away. Vermont, Colchester, the house on the lake. And the secret hiding place.

He backed out of the driveway with agonizing slowness, still managing to knock over a garbage can. A half mile down the street, he pulled into an abandoned strip mall. There, he drove the huge SUV in circles, building his confidence and skill.

Before getting on the turnpike, they stopped for gas. Aiden couldn't believe how easy this was when you had actual money to pay for it. Miguel still hadn't moved from the seat, but he had no problem buying their fuel. "Take it all," he mumbled, tossing wadded up bills at Aiden. "I don't want *anything* from Freddy."

While Aiden watched the attendant fill the tank, Meg invested in a road map at the mini-mart. They found Colchester near the top of Vermont, about three hundred and fifty miles away.

"Six hours' drive," Meg estimated. "If you don't wrap us around a telephone pole."

"Or get pulled over," Aiden added nervously.

It took them almost nine. Aiden missed a couple of exits, and his inexperience made it difficult to navigate back to the right road. A steady soaking rain began to fall, slowing them down further.

It was night by the time they reached the outskirts of Colchester. A 7-Eleven served as their pit stop for hot dogs and directions – a simple left towards the eastern shore of Lake Champlain. It was too dark to begin the search for the vacation house, so they pulled into a cheap motel for the night.

The desk clerk regarded Meg suspiciously. "I'll need your dad to come in and sign for the key."

"Oh, that's OK," she told him. "He gave me the money."

The old man shook his head. "State law. Got to be eighteen to check into a hotel, dear."

Meg thought fast. "OK, but if the baby wakes up, Dad's going to be mad. She's been crying since Yonkers, and we finally got her to sleep."

The clerk peered out the window at the Tahoe, which was being buffeted by sheets of blowing rain. He took a key from the drawer and placed it on the counter in front of Meg. "Room twenty-two," he said kindly. "There's a canopy by the soda machine so the baby won't get wet."

"Thanks, mister." Meg's big mouth had never let her down.

She hoped Aiden's memory was just as reliable.

The rain continued all night, playing a soft but persistent drumroll on the roof of the Olympia Motel. It did nothing to disturb the exhausted fugitives. This was their first night in real beds since Sunnydale. They slept like the dead.

But in the morning, Miguel began to examine their surroundings with a more critical eye. "This place is a hole, yo. You took me out of Jersey to come to this dump?"

121

"We took you out of Jersey because you wouldn't leave your brother's driveway," Meg shot right back.

Miguel was offended. "I was just chilling. I don't need help from anybody, least of all some *girl*!"

He had been gradually coming alive in the course of yesterday's drive. Now he was back to his old self. Meg liked him better sullen and silent.

There was little chance of that now. "Vermont, huh? I'm not impressed. Let's see if there's any action around." He was about to throw open the tattered curtains when he jumped back, cursing.

"What's wrong?" asked Aiden.

"Cops! And they're – oh, man. Not good!"

Aiden and Meg peered out the streaming glass. Two cruisers, lights flashing, and two uniformed officers to match. There was no question about it – they were heading towards—

"The car!" groaned Meg. "Can they tell it's stolen?"

"They can if the MacKinnons came home from Disney World," Aiden reasoned.

Miguel paced the small room like a caged tiger. "We gotta get out of here!"

Meg felt the panic rising inside her. *No escape through the front door. . .*

Then she saw it. "The bathroom!"

A narrow window led to the alley behind the motel. Aiden got there first. He leaped on to the toilet seat, flipped the latch, and pushed. "Stuck!"

Over the years, dozens of sloppy paint jobs had sealed the frame shut. Aiden pulled out the keys to the Tahoe and began to chisel at the layers of enamel.

"Hurry!" Meg urged tensely. One of the cops was on his way to the office.

In a minute, he'll know exactly where we are!

Aiden and Miguel grabbed the handle and pulled with all their strength.

And then the first cop was jogging back towards them. Meg heard him call to his partner, "Twenty-two!"

"Guys—"

There was a crack as the window jerked open. Miguel climbed on to the toilet tank and wiggled through the opening.

"Meg!" Aiden cried.

She didn't wait for an engraved invitation. She bolted into the bathroom a split second before the cops entered with their pass-key.

"Police! Freeze!"

But Meg wouldn't have stopped for a stampede of elephants. Aiden practically threw her out the window into the rain. She hit the ground, reached up, and pulled him through. He landed right on top of her. She felt her ankle twist, a stab of fire, as the two of them went down.

No time for pain. Not now...

And then the first officer was glaring at her through the glass.

"*Run!*" she yelled, hauling Aiden to his feet. They sprinted after Miguel, who was already halfway to the woods.

A quick glance over her shoulder. *Where are the cops?*

"Look!" Aiden pointed. The two officers were rounding the corner of the building in hot pursuit.

The Falconers blasted into the trees, pounding blindly through mud and wet underbrush. Bracken and low branches scratched at their faces and bodies, but they blundered on, not daring to slow down. A cry of shock rang out somewhere in front of them.

"Miguel?" Aiden panted.

Meg looked around desperately. There was nothing but trees and brush – and the rapid rustling of their own frenzied movements.

And then the forest floor disappeared beneath them.

She heard another scream – her own. The next

thing Meg knew, she was flat on her back, hurtling down a steep bluff towards the lakefront. Thirty-six hours of steady rain had converted the slope into a black diamond ski hill, coated with slick muck instead of snow.

She called to Aiden, just a few feet away, but no sound came out. Her words were sucked right back inside her, along with her breath, as she plunged ahead. She could see Miguel ahead of them, a slime-covered rocket sledge, racing wildly out of control.

Frantically, she tried to dig her arms into the grade to slow her descent. Instead, she accelerated. The tickly sensation of free fall – that roller-coaster feeling – took hold in her stomach.

But a roller coaster is a controlled drop! Who knows what's at the bottom of this slide? Rocks? A barbed wire fence? A brick wall?

Determinedly, she kicked a sneaker deep into the mud. All at once, her momentum halted. The world twisted violently, and she bounced head over heels, her slide now a roll. Lake Champlain became a spinning blur, and she lost all sense of where she was.

She cried, "Help!" Or maybe it was just her mind screaming as she tumbled towards—

Towards what?

Suddenly, it was all over. She was sprawled across the broken line of a paved road—

With a big pickup truck coming right at me!

Two sets of hands grabbed her wrists and yanked her up and out of the way just before the pickup roared past.

"You OK?" Aiden gasped, his face white behind a layer of sludge.

She nodded, gasping for breath. "Where are the cops?"

"We gotta disappear!" Miguel scouted the area. They were right at the shore – a small neighbourhood of docks and beach cottages. "This way!"

The Falconers had no choice but to follow. Surely the officers would be here soon. Or their colleagues would, answering a radio call to be on the lookout for three dazed and filthy kids.

Moving like a cat, Miguel led them to a small marina by the ferry pier. Without hesitation, he burrowed under the tarpaulin that covered the open stern of a sailing boat. He lifted the sheeting, beckoning Aiden and Meg to join him. The hatch was unlocked, and the three fugitives scrambled into the cramped cabin.

They were quite a sight – wild-eyed from the chase and caked with mud.

But we're safe, thought Meg. *For now, anyway.*

Aiden looked haunted. "I – I think I saw it," he rasped, struggling to catch his breath. "No – I'm sure of it."

"Saw what?" asked Miguel.

"The house – just past the ferry terminal on the lake side." He clasped his sister's hands, dribbling wet muck on the deck. "We made it, Meg. We're here."

17

Agent Harris knew it was a long shot. Still, in law enforcement, sometimes it was better to be lucky than smart.

SEARCH PARAMETERS: _____

He typed "Chicago", and then "three juveniles". The computer searched the FBI's database of crime reports from coast to coast. More than six hundred hits registered. Another waste of time.

He frowned. How had the Falconers avoided capture for so long? The Chicago police had been right on their tail. There were officers watching the airports, train stations and bus terminals. If the fugitives were still in that neighbourhood, surely they would have been found by now.

Of course, Aiden and Margaret were with the Reyes boy. He was a hardened criminal, with a rap sheet and a half. He might know a few tricks that wouldn't occur to a couple of professors' kids.

Hmmm...

Eyebrows raised, Harris added "stolen car" to the search keywords.

Suddenly, there it was – a 2003 Chevy Tahoe, taken from a suburban Chicago home and recovered at a motel in Colchester, Vermont. Officers there pursued three juveniles, who were still at large.

It was them. It had to be.

All the flights to Burlington, Vermont – near Colchester – were delayed because of high winds and heavy rain. Wherever the fugitives were hiding, they were probably soaked to the skin. The airline said it had been pouring up there for a day and a half. The National Weather Service was predicting no let-up in the storm.

Finally, a break. A friend in the military offered Agent Harris a seat on a helicopter transport to Ethan Allen Air Base on the west coast of Lake Champlain in upstate New York. From there, a one-hour ferry ride would take him straight into Colchester.

The flight was a nightmare. Howling winds blew

the chopper around like a kite. The ride was so bumpy that his entire Starbucks Extra-Dark Roast emptied itself on to his trousers, one slosh at a time. Agent Harris considered wasting good coffee a crime against humanity, but today he didn't mind. He was too airsick to drink it anyway.

He landed in Plattsburgh, New York, to find that all ferries to Vermont had been suspended due to the bad weather. Standing in the blowing rain in front of the locked ticket booth, he used language not at all becoming an agent of the United States government.

He was in luck, though. There was one rental car still available in the city of Plattsburgh – a Mini Cooper. He practically needed a shoehorn to cram his six-foot-seven frame into it.

The route around Lake Champlain would take him almost to the Canadian border, eighty miles out of his way.

Would the Falconer kids still be in Colchester by the time he got there?

The inside of the sailing boat had become a sauna. The tarpaulin sealed the air inside, making the cabin as stuffy as a tomb.

Aiden was too anxious to notice that it was impossible to breathe.

They were being hunted – there was no question about that. Police sirens – distant, yet not distant enough – wailed all day long. Car doors slammed and voices spoke over walkie-talkies. As the storm pounded Lake Champlain, the boat bobbed in the waves, jerking its mooring lines and bumping up against the dock. To Aiden, every jolt, every sound was the SWAT team, preparing to swoop down and arrest them.

Seasickness amplified their discomfort. When they got used to the motion, hunger came.

Miguel gazed bleakly around the small refrigerator. "What kind of people own this crate? They got food to put on food, but no food to put it on."

It was true. The tiny galley had plenty of condiments – ketchup, mustard and a hot sauce that claimed to be banned in thirteen states. Beyond that, there was nothing more than a half sleeve of mouldy crackers.

"Just be grateful they're not the kind of people who enjoy boating in the rain," Meg replied grimly.

By late afternoon, the sirens had ceased. In fact, there were very few sounds at all from the world outside the boat. Whatever vacationers were still around had given up on the day. With the ferries cancelled and the rain still going strong, the lakefront was deserted.

Even so, the fugitives waited until night had fallen before creeping out from under the tarpaulin.

Meg shuddered from the onslaught of blustery rain. "I was looking forward to getting out of that floating coffin. Now I'm ready to go back."

The summer house was smaller than Aiden remembered it, and the gleaming white paint had faded to a sort of air-pollution grey. But this was definitely the place. Same wooden shingles, same lamp-post mailbox, same makeshift boat dock out the back.

Getting in was Miguel's department. It took even less time than the MacKinnon home. He just pushed open a window, climbed inside, and helped Aiden and Meg in after him. "Hicks," he muttered. "They never lock anything."

Meg flicked the light switch. Nothing happened. She tried the one in the living room. Same result. "Power's off."

There was just enough glow from the street lamps to look around.

Aiden was mesmerized. *The outside may be differ-*

ent, but in here it's exactly like it was nine years ago.

Same shag carpeting. Same 1970s furniture. Even the muskie was there — a hideous two-foot-long open-mouthed fish mounted on a wooden plaque. It still held the place of honour in the foyer. Mom used to be so grossed out by the thing that she claimed she could actually smell it decomposing.

Miguel squinted in the gloom. "Kind of a dump, yo."

"Nothing worth stealing?" Meg asked sarcastically.

Miguel shrugged. "I thought you Falcons were high society."

"Our parents are college professors," Aiden told him. "You know, before. . ." His voice trailed off. "I'm going to find my old room."

"I'll go with you," said Meg.

"I'll check out the TV," Miguel decided. "Maybe they've got some DVDs we can fence."

Upstairs, the outside lamplight shone a dull orange through the dormer windows. It was claustrophobic — the A-frame roof cut the bedrooms in half. Aiden remembered it being so *big*.

"OK," Meg said. "Where's this famous hiding place?"

Aiden scanned the tiny room with anxious eyes.

133

Nine years was a long time. It was more than possible that someone had repaired the wall between then and now.

Funny – he had always known that. Yet right now the feeling that rose in him was close to panic.

If we can't find that picture, we're stuck. No leads, nowhere to go, no light at the end of the tunnel...

Being a fugitive wasn't fun, but at least they had some direction – the goal of saving their parents. If that turned out to be a dead end, they'd have nothing. They'd be wanderers. Worse, hunted animals.

Then he saw it. By the foot of the small desk, a square of panelling was attached at an odd angle. He dropped to his knees and began prying at it.

It didn't budge. Someone had nailed it into place. Had that person also removed his cigar box of treasures?

Can't think about that now...

"Help me," he said, and Meg joined him on the floor.

There was a cracking sound, and the piece broke away from the wall. Aiden peered into the hole. This was it – the moment of truth.

"Yes!"

The cigar box was faded and dust-covered. But it was exactly where six-year-old Aiden had left it.

Reverently, as if handling an ancient artefact, he took it out and opened the lid.

There were a few rusted bottle caps, a penny minted in 1916, and a yellowed book of matches from the Colchester Grill. A couple of toy soldiers and a small cluster of amethyst crystals he had once discovered on the underside of a stone.

"Not exactly the crown jewels," Meg commented dryly.

Most of all, there were pictures. *Terrible* pictures, although back then Aiden had been so proud of them. They were blurry and clumsily framed, with subjects' heads cut off and large pink fingers in the way.

But as Aiden flipped through the stack, he realized these *were* the crown jewels. No, much more valuable than that—

The photographs showed the most notorious traitors in half a century, Doctors John and Louise Falconer, laughing, posing, and playing with baby Meg.

Oh, God, was there really a time like this? A time before trials, and prisons, and foster homes, and the Department of Juvenile Corrections? Were we ever really this happy?

Meg was choked up, too. "I forgot how they look when they smile."

And then the picture was right before their eyes in the dim light: a man and a woman, clad in bathing suits, relaxing on a hotel pool deck. The man was pale and lean, with long reddish-brown hair and a full beard.

Uncle Frank. The man who had started in motion the series of events that destroyed the Falconer family.

The only person who could save them.

Miguel pulled the carton from the back of the closet and dumped out its contents. *Junk*, he thought, riffling through the pile of expired coupon books, broken swim goggles, single gloves, and cheap toys.

He stood on tiptoe and felt around the shelf. Something heavy bounced off his forehead and hit the carpet. What the—?

It was a thick hardback novel. He squinted at the cover in the dim light. *The Venus Flytrap Gambit – A Mac Mulvey Mystery*. At the bottom it said, *by John Falconer*.

Their father. He wasn't just a teacher; he was an author, too. Miguel remembered hearing something about that back when the Falconers first got busted. Not that Miguel was a news junkie, but you had to be deaf, dumb and blind to miss *that* story.

Were Aiden and Meg lying about not being rich? You sure couldn't tell by this house. But this wasn't their real crib. It was just somewhere they went for the summers.

"Rentals!" he spat in disgust. Little sis hit it right on the nose. There was nothing to rob in this dive. No cash, no jewellery – nothing worth the space it would take up in his pockets.

A noise startled him. He hadn't heard the others coming downstairs. "No offence," he added loudly. "I'm sure your family had some laughs in this—"

The face appeared out of the shadows. Chalky white skin on a completely shaved head.

A cop? Or some homeless guy who moved in when the summer people left?

"Yo, who are—?"

A large hand with the power of a robotic claw grabbed Miguel by the throat. He tried to yell for help, but no sound came out.

Miguel Reyes had been in many fights in his fifteen years. He had been picked on by his stepfather, by gang kids, and by inmates at three juvenile prisons. But he knew instantly that something was different now.

This assailant was no bully. He was an assassin.

He's trying to strangle me!

Unable to breathe or struggle free, Miguel felt around for a weapon. There was nothing – just *The Venus Flytrap Gambit*. His hand closed around the thick novel. It would have to do. Lack of oxygen was sapping his strength. His vision was darkening around the edges. It was now or never.

With all the force he could muster, he swung the book at the bald head, aiming the corner of the hardbound cover at the man's eye. There was a cry of pain. Miguel sucked in a huge breath as the constricting grip released his throat.

He tried to kick at his attacker, but the powerful hands caught his leg in mid-air and hurled Miguel into a bookcase. Magazines and cheap knick-knacks rained down on him.

"*Help!*" He realized right then how much he needed it. Whoever this bald guy was, he meant business.

Those two pampered kids upstairs were all that stood between Miguel and murder.

They heard the sounds of the struggle, followed by Miguel's muffled cry.

Aiden was instantly on his feet, stuffing the photograph into his pocket. "The cops!"

Meg looked around. The stairs were the only way out. Except – "The window!"

"What about Miguel?"

"We can't help him," Meg reasoned, remembering

Miguel's own logic at the truck stop. "If the cops have him, he's already done."

With effort, Aiden and Meg managed to get the window open and scramble out into the rain. The A-frame roof was so steep that Meg had to slither snake-style as she led the way to the overhang of the front porch. She let herself slide until she was able to wrap her arms and legs around the wooden post and shinny to the ground. An anxious moment later, Aiden jumped down beside her.

"Let's get out of here," hissed Meg.

"Wait." Aiden looked around. The lakefront was still deserted. "Do you see any police cars?"

"If we can walk, so can the cops," Meg argued.

"Yeah, but why would they?" Staying flush against the front of the house, Aiden peered in the window. From the outside, the interior seemed pitch-dark, but he could hear the bump and crash of slamming doors and toppling furniture.

A fight?

No, more like a chase through rooms and hallways. Miguel wasn't going down easily.

But why would he resist arrest when there's no hope?

"Where's the girl?" roared a man's voice.

"What did I do?" Tough Miguel's reply was a plaintive whimper.

140

"Where's your sister?" the voice demanded.

He thinks Miguel is me!

Then it happened. A sudden flash of yellow. A short, sharp crack.

Gunshot.

With Meg hot on his heels, Aiden barrelled in the front door just as the shooter moved to make his escape. There was an audible crunch as Aiden's forehead collided with the bald man's jaw. The pistol dropped to the floor of the foyer with a clatter. Aiden was jolted back into Meg, sending her sprawling on to the step.

The intruder recovered quickly and lashed out with a lightning fist. The hammer blow caught Aiden in the cheek, knocking him into the wall. His head struck something round and hard, and he saw stars. A rail?

No, it's the muskie! The preserved body was solid as granite.

"Get the gun!" cried Meg.

But Aiden was too slow. By the time he spotted the pistol on the linoleum, the attacker's hand was already closing on the grip.

The blast of terror was as cold as liquid nitrogen. In less than a second, the muzzle would swing up at Aiden, and his life would be over.

With a desperation and purpose he would not have believed possible, Aiden wrenched the mounted muskie off its wall hooks. Before the man could point the weapon, Aiden raised the trophy high and slammed it down on the side of his opponent's head.

The frame snapped in two. The assassin went rigid and dropped like a stone, out cold. The wood *and* the muskie itself landed on his unmoving back.

Mom always said this eyesore served no earthly purpose, Aiden reflected. *She was wrong.*

But there was no time to think about that now. "Miguel!" He hauled Meg to her feet, and the two of them stepped over the unconscious intruder and ran into the house, calling for their companion.

"In here," came a weak voice from the kitchen.

In the laundry alcove, Miguel lay propped against the washing machine. Even in the gloom, they could see his face was pale, almost ashen. Blood oozed from a bullet wound in his shoulder. The entire front of his T-shirt was stained crimson.

Aiden got under one shoulder, Meg the other, and they were able to hoist him to his feet. Miguel howled in agony at the sudden movement.

"We'll get you to a hospital," promised Aiden.

"What about Hairless Joe?"

"Forget him," soothed Meg.

"He had a *gun*!"

"I had a fish," Aiden replied.

Miguel saw his attacker prostrate on the floor with the fossilized muskie on his back. "You know this guy?"

Meg shook her head. "Do you?"

"Figured him for a cop. But cops don't whack people." He regarded Aiden. "This guy thought I was you. Somebody wants you dead. Both of you."

Aiden and Meg exchanged an uneasy look. Tens of thousands of people wished harm on their parents. But on *them*? It was hard to fathom.

"Maybe we should tie him up with the curtain cords," Meg suggested. "Make him tell us what's going on."

"We've got to get Miguel to a doctor," Aiden argued. "That's the most important thing."

"Take his piece at least," Miguel rasped. "He could come to any minute."

Aiden had never touched a gun in his life. He picked up the weapon with two fingers, handling it like a sleeping tarantula. The metal felt cold, malevolent. This was an instrument of evil, a delivery system for harm and death.

Once outside, he hurled it into Lake Champlain. It was a relief to be rid of it.

The relentless rain cranked Miguel's suffering beyond the tolerance level. There was simply no way to keep his shoulder dry. Aiden couldn't help noticing how much red-tinged water was dripping down from the bloodstained T-shirt.

He needs medical attention. And fast!

Heart sinking, Aiden looked for a house with some lights on. Why wasn't anybody home? Just then, a car turned on to the shore road, heading away from them.

"Wait here!" Aiden shrugged out from under Miguel and took off after the white Mercedes. "*Stop! Come back! My friend's hurt!*"

With the windows shut and the wipers on maximum, there was little chance of the driver hearing his cries.

Aiden broke into a full sprint, splashing through puddles that were more like ponds.

Don't be stupid! You can't outrun a car. You'll have to find some other way.

He dashed to the side of the road, scooped up a fistful of rain-drenched turf, and flung it with all his might at the receding sedan. It hit with a splat, showering mud and grass over the rear windshield and trunk.

Aiden had just an instant to consider that the owner of a gleaming white Mercedes probably wouldn't think much of being muck-bombed by a total stranger.

And then the brake lights flashed on.

It was well after dark by the time Agent Harris made it to Colchester. Because of the storm, the bridges across the top of Lake Champlain were closed. He'd had no choice but to drive all the way north around the lake. This included a one-hour wait at the Canadian border and another delay crossing back into the United States.

The wind had subsided, but the rain was still pouring down when he finally turned on to the main shore road. Suddenly, his headlights illuminated a running figure, dead ahead.

With a cry of shock, Harris stomped on the brake

pedal. The wheels locked up, sending the Mini Cooper in to a slide. At the last instant, the man vaulted up on to the front of the compact vehicle. He bounced off the hood and tumbled in to the windshield as the car lurched to a halt.

Harris caught a glimpse of him in the glow of the street lamp – a pale, round-faced man with a completely shaved head. Apparently, he was un-hurt, because he jumped off the hood and hit the road in a full sprint.

Harris rolled down his window. "*Hey, come back! You should see a doctor!*" he shouted at the fleeing form. But the man was gone, barrelling up the road that led away from the lake. He was in such a hurry that he probably never even noticed he'd nearly got himself killed.

That was when Harris heard the siren.

An ambulance screeched around the corner, its flashing lights playing across the ferry terminal like a disco ball. It raced up the road and stopped beside a white Mercedes.

Harris wheeled around and pulled even with the two vehicles. He nearly scrambled his brains against the Mini Cooper's door frame as he leaped out. But he recovered enough to flash his badge at the two paramedics. "Emmanuel Harris – FBI."

They were loading a thin olive-skinned teenager in a bloodstained T-shirt on to a stretcher.

"FBI?" The teen regarded the agent's lanky frame. "You look more like NBA."

"You're Reyes, right?" said Harris. "What happened?"

"I got shot. By some mean-looking bullet head straight out of some slasher flick."

"What about the Falconers?" the agent persisted. "A boy and a girl – they call themselves Eagleson—"

Miguel's jaw stiffened. "Don't know any eagles, falcons – no kinds of birds, yo."

The driver of the Mercedes spoke up. "It was two kids who flagged me down. They brought this one over, told me to call nine-one-one, and took off into the woods."

"How long ago?"

"Maybe ten minutes. They were in a real hurry to get out of here."

"He's lying!" rasped Miguel, determined to protect his friends. "I was alone, and some guy put a cap in me! If you cops spent less time hassling people, there wouldn't be so many wackos running around—"

"Quiet!" Harris snapped. Ten minutes! If those

bridges had been open . . . if the borders hadn't been so slow . . . if the ferries could have run. . .

If only he could have got here ten minutes sooner, those kids would be in custody right now. Instead of on the run, where anything could happen. Where they were risking their futures, their safety, their very *lives*, with every reckless footfall.

He was amazed at the depth of his emotions. Aiden and Margaret Falconer were not his problem. They weren't even his case. They were the responsibility of Adler and Juvenile Corrections, not the FBI.

Their *parents* had been Harris's case – case closed, and a job well done, too. The trial of the new millennium, two dangerous traitors behind bars.

And what did Harris get? A promotion, a pat on the back, and something else, too. Something agents weren't supposed to have.

A deep, nagging suspicion that the wrong people were in prison. And that two innocent children might be fugitives because of the government's haste to bring someone – *anyone* – to justice.

Well, at least that part would be over soon. With a sigh, he pulled out his mobile and dialled the Colchester police. Ten minutes wasn't much of a head start when you were travelling on foot.

They wouldn't get far.

The ATV was a quad, with four fat wheels and an engine that might have been built for a jumbo jet. The speedometer said they were doing better than fifty over rugged terrain, bouncing like riders on a mechanical bull. Aiden had all but glued himself to the handlebars; Meg was clamped around his mid-section with force enough to collapse his ribcage. The onslaught of wind and rain threatened to hurl them off the speeding contraption at any moment.

The roar should have been enough to attract every cop in Vermont. But that was the advantage of the ATV. They were cutting across farms and fields, far from any roads or highways.

Another crime – was there such a thing as "grand theft dune buggy"? The scary part was not so much that they'd stolen it; Aiden had lost track of the number of times they had broken the law by now. It was the fact that they never thought twice about taking the quad from that garage.

We had to get out of town. And even more important: *we had to get away from Hairless Joe.*

Yesterday, Aiden couldn't have imagined their predicament getting any worse. But the close call with the monstrous bald stranger had ratcheted their fear up to a new, soul-shaking level. Before, the worst thing that could have happened to them was getting caught.

Now somebody wants us dead.

But who? Why? And how had he found them at the lake house?

They had been in full flight for a couple of hours when the old barn appeared in the ATV's single headlamp. It came up so suddenly that they almost crashed through the rotted plank walls. Aiden yanked the handlebars around. For an awful instant, he thought the speeding vehicle would roll. But the huge wheels bit into the turf, and Aiden and Meg whiplashed to a halt six inches in front of an ancient rusted tractor.

Aiden aimed the quad's light into the barn, and they hurried inside to shelter from the elements. The storm had brought down the temperature, so they were both soaked to the skin and shivering.

"I can't stop shaking," Aiden managed, teeth

chattering. "Is summer over already? What's it going to be like being a fugitive in January?"

"I'd still be shaking in a sauna," Meg said feelingly. "Who was that guy, and why was he trying to kill us?"

Aiden shrugged. "The whole country hates our parents. I guess it was only a matter of time before somebody tried to take it out on us."

"How do you know it wasn't just bad luck?" Meg suggested hopefully. "You know, a crazy person who picked a house at random."

Aiden shook his head. "He was gunning for us. He even said, 'Where's your sister?' when he thought Miguel was me."

"Miguel." She nodded sadly. "I hope he's OK."

"He got hit in the shoulder, which means the bullet missed the vital organs." Aiden paused, suddenly thoughtful. "I hated that kid more than I hated Sunnydale. More than what happened to us, almost. Now I feel like I've lost a brother. I mean, he's not dead, but he's caught. He's going back into the system."

After the frantic commotion at the house and the clamour of the ATV, the quiet between them was as jarring as a sonic boom. Both knew what "back into the system" represented for Miguel. Not another place like Sunnydale, but real jail, with bars and armed guards and inmates who could teach Miguel the true meaning of tough.

At last, Meg put an arm around her brother's shoulders. "We're still kicking, bro. That's the important thing. What's our next move?"

Carefully, Aiden pulled the soggy, partially crumpled photograph out of his pocket. It seemed even more bizarre in this setting – to be huddled in the headlamp of a stolen ATV in an abandoned barn, studying a nine-year-old image of two strangers sunbathing.

Uncle Frank, who could straighten everything out. The key to it all.

The despair was completely unexpected. One minute he was examining the photograph; the next, he was staring into a bottomless pit of desolation.

I was nuts to think this picture could somehow help our parents. I don't recognize this guy, and even if I did, so what? Does he even look like this today?

Aiden felt completely deflated. What did he expect? That one glance at this snapshot would tell him how to get in touch with the man who held the family's fate in his hands? Did he imagine Lindenauer would be holding up a sign with his contact information on it – WWW.CALLUNCLEFRANK.COM?

I must have been out of my mind to risk our lives crossing the entire country for a dumb old picture that doesn't give the slightest clue—

And then he saw it.

Above the reclining figures, almost out of frame, a life jacket was mounted on the slats of the pool area fence. Printed on the white plastic ring, small but clear, was:

RED JACKET BEACH MOTOR LODGE
MALLET'S BAY, VERMONT

Meg noticed it, too. "It's only the name of the hotel," she pointed out.

Aiden's heart began to pound "Yeah, but hotels have computers. They keep records. Addresses, phone numbers. . ."

"It's a clue," she agreed grudgingly.

At that moment, Aiden realized that he and his sister were not ordinary fugitives. Fugitives ran *away* from justice. The Falconers were running *towards* it.

As long as there was a place to start, a lead to follow, a stone left unturned in the quest to prove their parents' innocence, then there was hope.

153

He peered out of the barn. In the blinding light of the headlamp, everything else appeared dark.

Somewhere, he thought, *in that vast blackness between here and the end of the earth, is Frank Lindenauer.*

They would find him.